THE EVIL IS BACK.

Amanda shoved her cheerleading uniform into her bag and put her pompoms in her locker.

As she started to shut the locker door, she noticed something stuffed way at the back of the narrow shelf. She reached in and pulled out a pale blue duffel bag.

A name tag hung from one of the straps. Amanda turned it over. "Corky Corcoran," she read aloud. "Where have I heard that name?"

Curious, she sat on the bench and unzipped the bag. Inside, neatly folded, was a cheerleading uniform.

A Shadyside uniform, Amanda thought. An old one.

"Amanda, are you ready?" Victoria called from the next aisle.

"Just a sec." As Amanda started to stuff the old uniform back into the bag, she noticed something else inside. She reached in and pulled it out.

It was a small box, made of smooth, dark wood. A tarnished brass catch held the lid closed.

A label had been taped to the top of the box, with bold black letters that screamed out a warning:

DO NOT OPEN. EVIL INSIDE.

Books by R.L. Stine

Available from ARCHWAY Paperbacks

FEAR STREET®

R·L·STINE

SUPER CHILLER

CHEERLEADERS
The Evil Lives!

A Parachute Press Book

AN ARCHWAY PAPERBACK
Published by POCKET BOOKS
New York London Toronto Sydney Tokyo Singapore

AN ARCHWAY PAPERBACK *Original*

An Archway Paperback published by
POCKET BOOKS, a division of Simon & Schuster Inc.
1230 Avenue of the Americas, New York, NY 10020

Copyright © 1998 by Parachute Press, Inc.

ISBN: 0-671-52972-2

First Archway Paperback printing January 1998

10 9 8 7 6 5 4 3

FEAR STREET is a registered trademark of Parachute Press, Inc.

AN ARCHWAY PAPERBACK and colophon are registered trademarks of Simon & Schuster Inc.

Cover art by Lisa Falkenstern

Printed in the U.S.A.

IL 7+

PART ONE

Chapter 1

FIRST SCREAM

*A*manda Roberts pulled her thick, auburn hair up into a ponytail and wrapped a rubber band around it. Then she curved one arm over her head and bent sideways from the waist. "Ugh!" she groaned. "I'm as stiff as a piece of dry spaghetti."

Janine Klein, Amanda's best friend, blew out a breath and started in on some leg stretches. "Don't even mention food," she pleaded. "All I've done this whole Christmas vacation is feed my face. If I eat one more piece of fudge, I'll pop out of my uniform."

Keesha Wilson grinned and her hazel eyes sparkled. "That would give the crowd something to cheer about!" she exclaimed.

Amanda laughed and continued her exercises. It was Saturday. School started Monday, so she'd called a cheerleading practice. Amanda, a senior at Shady-side High, was captain of the squad.

It's the best squad in years, she thought, glancing around at the four other cheerleaders.

Janine was short and slightly stocky, with a round face and big brown eyes. She always complained about her weight, but she was as light on her feet as anybody.

Tiny Keesha Wilson had tons of energy. Plus she was always laughing and joking. Nobody ever got too serious when Keesha was around.

Nobody except Natalie Morris. Amanda paused for a second and watched Natalie practice a spread eagle, jumping high off the floor with her legs straight out. Slender and graceful, with dark hair and gray eyes, Natalie was shy and quiet and very serious. She only came alive when she was cheerleading.

Victoria Hopewell stood near Natalie, practicing some kicks. The two of them were good friends, which was weird because they were so different. Victoria was big-boned and athletic, and as friendly as a puppy. She had the most spirit of anyone on the squad.

As Amanda went back to her warm-ups, the gym door burst open, and the boys' basketball team ran onto the other end of the court. The Tigers had their first game against Lincoln on Friday.

"Andrew!" Keesha shouted, jumping up and down and waving. "Don't forget—we're going out to eat after practice!"

Andrew Collins flashed Keesha a thumbs-up, then turned back to his teammates.

Janine nudged Amanda in the side. "I'll bet you a hundred dollars they never get around to eating," she whispered.

4

Amanda rolled her eyes and nodded. Keesha was totally obsessed with Andrew. "Come on, Keesha!" she yelled. "Finish your warm-ups!"

"But Andrew is so awesome looking, I can't help staring!" Keesha protested with a giggle. She began her warm-ups again.

Amanda smiled. Every cheerleader except Victoria had a boyfriend on the team. So it *was* kind of hard to concentrate sometimes when they were all together.

Janine went with Brandon Farr, a wiry, red-haired forward who liked to joke as much as Keesha. Natalie dated cool, blond-haired Luke Stone, another forward. And Amanda was going with Dustin Feld.·

Amanda gazed down the court at Dustin. His sandy hair flopped around his head as he leaped into the air and shot at the basket. The ball circled the rim three times, then fell off. Dustin angrily grabbed it up and spiked it on the floor.

Amanda sighed. Why can't he lighten up? she wondered. Why does he have to be so intense?

"Check out Brandon!" Janine cried. "Does he look good or what?"

Amanda glanced down the court. Brandon raced toward the basket and got ready to shoot. But at the last second, Luke Stone snatched the ball from his hands, turned, leaped, and sank the shot.

Natalie punched her fist into the air and shot Janine a cool, superior smile.

Amanda sighed again. Luke and Brandon were competing to be on the starting team on Friday, and their rivalry had rubbed off on their girlfriends. Especially on Natalie.

Natalie is another one who needs to lighten up,

Amanda thought. She could cause problems on the squad if she keeps treating Janine like a rival.

As Amanda tried to decide whether she should discuss this rivalry with Natalie, a basketball bounced across the floor and rolled to a stop in front of her feet. She picked it up, bounced it a couple of times, and heaved it down the court.

Judd Hunter, the Tigers' center, grabbed it out of the air and grinned at her. "Nice throw!" he yelled. "You have a better arm than I do!"

Amanda felt herself blush. She hadn't told anyone, but she'd had a crush on Judd for a month now. Not only was he a great player, he was a great-looking player. Dark hair, sky-blue eyes, broad shoulders, and high cheekbones.

Plus he played basketball as if it were the most fun thing in the world—not a heavy-duty chore, the way Dustin did.

Dustin treated *everything* like a chore. Or a test. Amanda still liked him okay, but not as a boyfriend. It's time to find a new boyfriend for the new year, she thought. Time to move on.

Maybe on to Judd Hunter.

A shrill whistle broke into Amanda's thoughts as Miss Daly, the cheerleading coach, entered the gym.

Amanda smiled to herself. Tall and gangly, with red-orange hair swept up into a messy topknot, Miss Daly reminded her of an ostrich.

"Time to get to work," the coach declared as she stopped in front of the cheerleaders. "Amanda, the walkovers in the new routine could use some polishing, don't you think?"

"Right," Amanda agreed. "Okay, everybody, line

up. Keesha and Victoria, start your walkovers on the word 'prowl.'"

The cheerleaders arranged themselves in a straight line, arms stretched out, fingers almost touching.

> *"Hey, Lincoln, don't look now,*
> *The Shadyside Tigers are on the prowl!"*

On the beat, Keesha and Victoria began their walkovers. As they straightened up and prepared for the next ones, a loud shout echoed off the gym walls.

Everyone turned to look. Amanda gasped.

At the other end of the court, Brandon and Luke were on the floor, wrestling furiously with each other. The other players gathered around.

"What's with you, man?" Brandon shouted hoarsely. "You think I need to trip you to get the starting position?"

"That's exactly what I think!" Luke shouted back. "The only way you'll get it is if I break my leg!"

Miss Daly blew her whistle and began loping down the floor, her topknot bobbing up and down.

"You're crazy!" Brandon cried. He flipped Luke onto his back and raised his fist.

With a shriek, Natalie raced down the floor, passing Miss Daly. "Stop it!" she cried, grabbing Brandon's arm. "You're the one who's crazy!"

Brandon gazed up at her in surprise. He shook her hand off and rose to his feet.

As Natalie reached out to help Luke up, several of the other players snickered. "What's the matter, Luke?" one of them teased. "Need your girlfriend to rescue you?"

Luke's pale face turned red with embarrassment. Ignoring Natalie's outstretched hand, he scrambled up and straightened his T-shirt. "I can take care of myself, Natalie," he mumbled.

"All right, *children,*" Miss Daly said sarcastically. "I suggest both of you grow up fast, before Coach Davis gets back here."

Brandon shrugged and turned away. Luke scowled for a second, then knelt down to tie a shoelace.

Natalie started to kneel beside him, but Miss Daly stopped her. "Come along, Natalie," she ordered. "Back to work."

Natalie followed the coach, frowning angrily. "That Brandon is such a creep!" she declared as she joined the rest of the squad. "He should be kicked off the team."

Uh-oh. Natalie really shouldn't bad-mouth Janine's boyfriend like that, Amanda thought.

She glanced at Janine. Her friend looked ready to explode. "Okay, everybody!" Amanda said quickly. "Let's take it from the top."

The five cheerleaders arranged themselves in a line and began the routine.

> *"Hey, Lincoln, don't look now,*
> *The Shadyside Tigers are on the prowl!*
> *Hey, Lincoln, better watch your back,*
> *The Shadyside Tigers are on the attack!"*

As they worked on the cheer, Amanda kept sneaking glances at Natalie and Janine. Thank goodness, she thought. They're too busy concentrating to think about each other or their boyfriends.

* * *

After an hour, Miss Daly finally blew her whistle. "Not bad," she announced. The cheerleaders gathered around, breathing hard. "Now what about the game next Friday? What other routines do you want to do at halftime?"

"We're getting together Sunday to decide," Amanda told her.

Miss Daly nodded. "See you in school on Monday," she said, then jogged across the gym to her little glass-fronted office.

"Who's hungry?" Victoria demanded, glancing around at the other cheerleaders. "Let's all go to The Corner."

"Not me." Keesha grinned. "Andrew and I have plans."

"I'm waiting here." Natalie unclipped her dark hair and shook it out. "For Luke," she added.

"I'll come," Amanda said. "I could use a pitcher of Coke."

"Me too," Victoria declared. "And some fries."

"And a shake," Janine added. "Chocolate."

Amanda laughed. "I thought you were worried about popping out of your uniform."

"Okay, so I'll have a *small* shake!" Janine tucked her chin-length brown hair behind her ears and stuck her tongue out.

Amanda crossed to the bleachers for her duffel bag. She slung it over her shoulder and turned around.

Judd Hunter stood in front of her. "Hi."

Amanda quickly wiped the sweat from her forehead and smiled. "Hi. Is your practice over, too?"

Judd shook his head. "We're just on a break." He smiled. His blue eyes crinkled at the corners.

9

Amanda's stomach did a little flip. He's so cute! she thought.

"I caught the end of your routine," Judd told her. "You looked really good."

Me? Amanda wondered. Or all of us? "Thanks," she said. "Have Brandon and Luke declared a truce?"

Before Judd could answer, a piercing scream rang out, echoing off the walls of the gym.

Amanda turned quickly.

Why was Janine on her knees in the middle of the floor?

Why was she opening her mouth in another scream of horror?

Chapter 2

EVIL APPEARS

"What is it?" Amanda shouted, rushing toward her friend. "Janine! Are you hurt? What happened?"

Janine leaped to her feet and pointed a shaking finger at her duffel bag. "Somebody—take it away!" she cried hysterically.

"What?" Victoria demanded. "What are you talking about?"

"That!" Janine kept pointing at her blue bag. "I can't stand those things. I can't *stand* them!"

Amanda skidded to a stop, her sneakers squeaking on the wooden floor, and peered down at the bag. "I don't see . . ." She broke off and gave a little gasp.

Inside the bag, on top of Janine's red sweater, lay a thin black snake.

As Amanda stared, it began to uncoil itself. Its flat,

wedge-shaped head slid over the zipper. Its forked tongue slithered out, flicking the air.

"Whoa!" Keesha cried. "Where did that come from?"

"The student parking lot," someone replied.

Everybody turned.

Brandon stood a few feet away, a mischievous gleam in his pale gray eyes. As everyone stared at him, he grinned. "Got you—didn't I, Janine?"

Janine glared at him. "I don't believe it! You put that horrible creature in my bag?"

"I believe it," Natalie muttered, shaking her head in disgust.

Amanda did, too. Putting a snake in someone's duffel bag was exactly the kind of prank Brandon loved to pull.

"How could you *do* that?" Janine demanded. "You scared me to death!"

"Oh, come on," Brandon protested. "When I found it outside, I couldn't resist."

"Guess what? I'm not laughing," Janine snapped. "I'm really tired of your dumb jokes, Brandon."

"Aw, give me a break. I'll get rid of it." Giving Janine an innocent, little-boy smile, Brandon trotted over to the duffel bag and picked up the snake. It froze for a second, then began to writhe wildly in his hand.

Janine took a step back, sucking in her breath.

Brandon chuckled. "Don't be scared. It's totally harmless. See?" He quickly thrust his arm out, pushing the snake an inch from Janine's face.

"Cut it out!" Janine shouted, stumbling backward.

"Okay, okay." Brandon spun around and lobbed the snake through the air.

12

Amanda ducked as the snake sailed over her head, straight toward Judd.

With a startled cry, Judd stuck his hand up and caught it.

"Come on, Judd!" Brandon cried, waving his arms over his head. "Toss it back!"

"Whoa, this thing can *move!*" Judd held the wriggling snake at arm's length.

"Throw it!" Brandon shouted.

Judd swung his arm back, then tossed the snake toward Brandon's outstretched hands.

Brandon leaped into the air and caught it above his head. "Yes! A perfect catch!" he yelled. "Okay, Judd—get ready!"

Before Brandon could throw the snake again, Natalie dove over and caught hold of his arm. "Stop throwing that poor thing around like it was made out of rubber," she scolded. "It's a living creature—not a toy."

"Come on, Natalie," Brandon said. "We weren't hurting it."

Natalie glared at him. "How do you know? Give it to me. I'll take it back outside where it belongs."

Brandon grinned sheepishly and handed over the snake. Shaking her head, Natalie marched across the gym toward the outside doors.

Janine gave Brandon a dirty look, then turned to Amanda. "Come on. Let's go get something to eat."

I'd rather talk to Judd some more, Amanda thought.

Unfortunately, Coach Davis returned and called the team back to practice.

With a sigh, Amanda grabbed her duffel bag and

followed Janine and Victoria into the girls' locker room.

"I'm absolutely going to kill Brandon," Janine muttered in a muffled voice as she pulled her T-shirt over her head.

"You always say that," Victoria reminded her. She sat on a bench in front of the lockers and unzipped her bag. "Every time he plays a trick, you threaten to kill him."

"This time I mean it."

Amanda laughed. "You do not." She walked down the aisle until she came to locker 312. Its battered door sagged crookedly, held up by only one hinge. "Oh, right," she murmured. "They assigned me a new locker."

Amanda fished a slip of paper out of her bag and checked the new locker number—113. She found it in the next aisle and pulled it open.

A small mirror hung on the inside of the door. Amanda checked her reflection. Strands of auburn hair had sprung loose from the rubber band, and her face was all sweaty and red from practicing so hard.

Great, she thought. I was certainly looking my best in front of Judd.

Shaking her head, she dressed in the jeans and yellow sweater she'd brought from home. She stuffed her practice clothes into her duffel, then brushed out her hair in front of the little mirror.

As she started to shut the locker door, she noticed something stuffed way at the back of the narrow shelf. She reached in and pulled out a pale blue duffel bag.

A name tag hung from one of the straps. Amanda turned it over. "Corky Corcoran," she read aloud. "Where have I heard that name?"

Curious, she sat on the bench and unzipped the bag. Inside, neatly folded, was a cheerleading uniform. A short, maroon-and-white skirt, and a thick white sweater with a big maroon "S" on the front.

A Shadyside uniform, Amanda thought. An old one. Now the squad wore one-piece uniforms with short, flared skirts and long sleeves.

As Amanda set the uniform aside, a photograph slid from its folds and fluttered to the floor. Amanda picked it up.

Five girls smiled out at her, all dressed in the old Shadyside cheerleading uniforms and holding maroon-and-white pompoms in the air.

"Amanda, are you ready?" Victoria called from the next aisle.

"Just a sec." As Amanda started to stuff the old uniform back into the bag, she noticed something else inside. She reached in and pulled it out.

It was a small box, made of smooth, dark wood. A tarnished brass catch held the lid closed.

A label had been taped to the top of the box, with bold black letters that screamed out a warning:

DO NOT OPEN. EVIL INSIDE.

Chapter 3

CORKY'S LETTER

"It has to be a joke," Victoria declared.

"You think so?" Amanda asked.

"Pretty creepy joke!" Janine ate a French fry, then took a sip of her shake.

The three of them sat at a booth in the little restaurant called The Corner, staring at the wooden box.

DO NOT OPEN. EVIL INSIDE.

Amanda shivered. The warning seemed to glare up at her.

She gestured at the photograph that had been in the duffel bag. "Does anybody know which cheerleader is Corky Corcoran?"

"That one," Victoria replied, pointing at the pretty blond-haired girl in the center.

"Did you know her?" Amanda asked.

Victoria shook her head. "I think she was cheer-leading captain when we were freshmen. Or maybe when we were still in middle school. Why?"

Amanda shrugged. "I just wondered if she was the kind of person who liked to joke around."

"Who cares?" Victoria said. "Let's open the box. I'm dying to find out what's inside."

Victoria is always ready to do anything, Amanda thought. "What about the warning?" she asked.

"Oh, please!" Victoria rolled her eyes. "Aren't you guys curious?"

"Well . . . sure." Amanda reached for the box.

Janine sucked in her breath.

Amanda quickly drew her hand back, laughing nervously.

Clicking her tongue with impatience, Victoria grabbed the box and unhooked the brass catch. "Get ready for the Evil!" she cried.

With a wicked cackle, Victoria lifted the lid.

Amanda held her breath. She knew it was silly, but she half expected some horrible, fiendish monster to rise from the box like a genie from a bottle.

But nothing happened.

Amanda cautiously peered inside.

On the bottom of the box lay a small stack of papers, tightly folded.

Victoria laughed. "Not exactly evil-looking, are they?"

"Maybe it's an old test that Corky failed," Janine suggested. "Or a break-up letter from some guy."

Amanda pulled out the first piece of paper and unfolded it. "It *is* a letter," she said. She turned it over and read the signature. "From Corky."

"Well? Don't keep us in suspense," Victoria told her. "Read it!"

Amanda cleared a space on the table, then smoothed the letter out and began to read:

"If you are reading this letter, then you've opened the box. I left it here as a warning. *Please!* Once you've finished reading, *destroy this box and everything in it!*"

Amanda glanced up.

"Keep going," Victoria urged.

"This is a story of Evil," Amanda read. "A horrible, terrifying Evil. An Evil that kills and kills and kills.

"And it's a true story. It happened to me and my friends.

"It all started at the Fear Street Cemetery. At the grave of a woman named Sarah Fear. Sarah died a hundred years ago. But the Evil that possessed her lived on."

Amanda shivered. This didn't sound like a joke.

"When I first became a Shadyside cheerleader," Corky's letter went on, "the squad was traveling to an away game. The bus skidded and crashed into the cemetery. Jennifer, one of the cheerleaders, was thrown out the window.

"She landed on Sarah Fear's grave.

"We didn't know it then, but that was the beginning.

"The Evil was released.

"And it took over Jennifer's body. Using Jennifer, it tried to kill me, to bury me in Sarah Fear's grave.

"I fought it. I thought I killed it. But I was wrong. The Evil was too strong, and it came back. This time, it came back in my friend, Kimmy. Next, it took over my body."

18

Amanda glanced up again.

Janine and Victoria sat still, serious expressions on their faces.

"This is really spooky," Janine murmured.

Victoria nodded wordlessly.

Amanda's heart pounded. The letter frightened her, and she wanted to rip it to pieces. But she couldn't stop reading.

"The Evil killed people in horrible, gruesome ways.

"It chopped off my boyfriend's hand and he bled to death.

"It forced a cheerleader to keep doing back flips, over and over and over, until she went crazy."

Victoria shuddered.

"I finally discovered a way to kill it," Amanda read, her voice shaking. "It had to be drowned. And I did it. I almost drowned, too. But I managed to kill the Evil.

"Is it *really* dead?

"I don't know."

Amanda paused.

"Is that it?" Janine whispered.

"No, there's a little more." Amanda licked her lips. "You may think this is a joke," she read. "I wish it was. But it isn't. The Evil lived. It killed. If it isn't really dead, it will kill again. *Destroy this box!"*

Chapter 4

THE EVIL SPEAKS

*A*manda stopped reading.

"Whoa," Janine murmured. "Talk about creepy!"

Amanda nodded and picked up her Coke. Her hand shook. She quickly put the glass down. "Maybe we should do what Corky says—destroy the box."

"Do you believe the letter?" Janine asked.

"I'm not sure," Amanda admitted. "What about you?"

"It's almost too weird to believe," Janine replied. "But there's something about it. I don't know—it sounds so serious. It's obviously not a joke."

"Yeah, Corky believes it, that's for sure," Victoria declared. "Maybe she went crazy and actually thought this Evil went around possessing people."

"Maybe." Amanda frowned. "But what about all those deaths?"

Victoria shrugged. "If Corky was crazy, maybe when somebody died, she decided the Evil did it."

"I guess you could be right," Amanda agreed. She eyed the box. "Do you think I should get rid of it?"

"Wait. At least let's see what the other papers are." Victoria started to reach for the box, then paused as a shadow fell across the table.

Amanda glanced up.

Dustin stood there, gazing down at her with an annoyed expression on his face.

Amanda forced a smile, even though she wasn't thrilled to see him. "Hi."

"Hi." Without waiting for an invitation, Dustin squeezed into the booth, forcing Amanda to slide over. "I searched for you after practice," he told her. "Why didn't you tell me where you were going?"

Amanda frowned. "I didn't think I had to."

"You don't." Dustin slipped an arm around her shoulders and pulled her close. "But I thought you'd want to," he added, nuzzling her neck.

Amanda glanced across the table. Victoria grinned. Janine rolled her eyes. This is so embarrassing, Amanda thought. Why does Dustin have to act like he owns me?

"Well, it doesn't matter now, right?" Dustin murmured, his lips against her ear. "I found you."

Janine cleared her throat loudly. "Guess what, Dustin? There are two other people at the table."

Amanda shrugged Dustin's arm off and straightened up. "How did the rest of practice go?" she asked.

"Great. The basketball part, anyway," Dustin replied. He grabbed a fry from Victoria's plate and chomped it down. "But you should have stayed. You missed the fireworks afterward."

Victoria propped her elbows on the table. "What happened?" she asked eagerly.

Dustin gave a snort of disgust. "Luke and Brandon got into it again. What else?"

Janine frowned. "You mean another fight?"

Dustin nodded. "They both want to start against Lincoln Friday night. The whole thing has turned into a major battle."

"Who started it this time?" Amanda asked.

"Hard to tell. Brandon laughed because Luke missed a free throw. According to Brandon, he was laughing at something else." Dustin shrugged. "Anyway, as soon as practice was over, they started pushing each other around. Then Luke threw a punch. He missed, but Brandon punched back. And Luke wound up with a bloody nose."

Janine gasped. "What happened then?"

"Luke went nuts. He plowed into Brandon and tackled him to the floor," Dustin continued. "It was a real mess—blood all over the place. And then Natalie got into it again."

"Whoa." Victoria sighed. "Natalie to the rescue."

"Yeah, she was screaming at the top of her lungs. Coach Davis finally came out of his office and broke it up."

Dustin grabbed another fry and slid out of the booth. "Come on," he said to Amanda. "I'll give you a ride home."

"I have my own car." Amanda started to tell him good-bye, then changed her mind. "But I'll walk you to yours," she added. Now is as good a time as any to break up with him, she thought. Get it over with, and you'll feel a lot happier.

Amanda stood up, fished the money for her Coke out of her bag, and said good-bye to her friends.

Outside, Dustin draped an arm across her shoulders. "Want to walk around a little?"

"Sure." It'll give me time to figure out exactly what to say, Amanda thought.

It had snowed a few days before. Today had been sunny, warm enough to turn the frozen ground to slush. But as Amanda tried to think of a good way to break up with Dustin, she shivered.

Dustin immediately tightened his arm around her. "What's wrong? It's not very cold."

"I know." Amanda sighed, feeling uncomfortable.

They walked past Dustin's car, to the end of the block. As they stopped at the corner, Dustin turned Amanda toward him and kissed her.

Amanda pulled away.

"What's the matter with you?" he demanded, gripping her shoulders. "You're acting weird. And you're so quiet."

"I'm just . . . thinking," Amanda replied.

"About what?" Dustin gazed at her and suddenly frowned. "What were you and Judd talking about at practice, anyway?"

"Nothing. Just stuff." Amanda took a deep breath. "But Dustin, I think you and I should just be friends."

Oh great, she told herself. Just blurt it right out, why don't you? "I mean, I think we should go out with other people."

Dustin dropped his hands and stared at her.

"I'm sorry," Amanda told him. "I didn't mean to say it like that."

Dustin kept staring at her, his eyes totally blank. No expression on his face. No reaction at all.

Like he's made of stone, Amanda thought with a shudder. "Dustin? Say something."

Dustin stood still. Frozen.

"Say *something*, please," Amanda cried. "You're *scaring* me!"

Dustin stared for a moment longer. Finally, his thin face relaxed. But his eyes remained blank, and icy cold.

"Dustin?"

"Whatever," he murmured in a hollow voice. He brushed past her without another word and walked casually back toward his car.

In spite of the warm afternoon sun, Amanda felt chilled to the bone. It would have been better if he'd gotten angry and yelled, she thought. Or argued with me. Or at least acted upset.

Anything would have been better than that blank, frozen stare.

Dustin's car pulled away from the curb. Amanda hurried back to The Corner to tell Janine what had happened.

Their booth was empty, though. Janine and Victoria had left.

Still feeling shaken, Amanda climbed into her car and drove home.

In her room, she dropped her bag on the floor, picked up the bedside phone, and punched in Janine's number.

A busy signal.

Probably talking to Brandon, Amanda thought. Which means she'll be on the phone for hours.

Sighing impatiently, Amanda hung up and glanced around. Her duffel bag lay crumpled in the middle of the floor. She should wash her gym shorts and socks and T-shirt. She didn't have any more clean ones.

As Amanda pulled her sweaty practice clothes from the bag, she remembered the wooden box with the papers folded in it.

Evil Inside, the warning had said. Maybe the papers explained what it was all about.

Amanda yanked out her shorts and a dirty yellow towel and peered into the bag.

At the bottom lay a couple of rubber bands and a half-eaten candy bar.

Nothing else.

The wooden box with its strange, frightening warning was gone.

Amanda pawed through her practice clothes. Maybe the box was wrapped up in them.

No.

It was definitely missing.

Amanda sat back on her heels. I must have left it at The Corner. Great. Now I'll never know what the rest of those papers said.

As Amanda gathered up her clothes, the phone rang. Janine, she thought. Now I can tell her about Dustin. She dropped the clothes in a heap and snatched up the phone. "Hello?"

A soft breath came across the line.

Amanda frowned. "Janine?"

Another breath. And then a low, husky whisper. "Amanda."

Amanda's skin prickled. "Yes? Who is this?"

"This is the evil spirit, Amanda," the low voice whispered.

Amanda's heart began to thud.

"I'm alive," the voice continued. "I didn't drown. I'm coming for you."

Chapter 5

AN EVIL PLAN

*A*manda clutched the phone tightly, picturing the warning on the box.

When we opened it up, did we actually let out some kind of evil? she asked herself.

"Watch out, Amanda," the voice whispered. "Watch out before you fall for another joke like this one because I'll tell everyone at Shadyside High!"

Huh? Amanda pulled the receiver away and stared at it. She knew that voice. She clapped the phone to her ear. "Keesha!"

"Wow! Were you slow to catch on!" Keesha cried as she burst out laughing. "Hel-lo! Earth calling Amanda! I really had you fooled, didn't I?"

Amanda sank onto the bed, embarrassed. But relieved, too.

"Okay, you fooled me," she admitted with a grin. "I should have known it was you. But wait—how did *you* know about Corky's letter?"

"Janine took the little box with her when she left The Corner," Keesha explained. "She called me up a few minutes ago and told me all about it."

"Scary, huh?"

"Weird, you mean. And the other papers inside— somebody had a really twisted sense of humor."

"Janine read them? What did they say?"

"They're instructions on how to call up the evil spirit. Can you believe it?" Keesha asked.

Amanda felt her skin prickle again. "I wish I'd never found that box," she declared.

"Oh, come on. It's kind of fun," Keesha replied. "And you know what? We should do it."

"Do what?"

"Call up the evil spirit," Keesha declared. "We have the instructions, right? Why not?"

"What a horrible idea," Amanda told her. "What if—"

Keesha snorted. "Don't get all superstitious, Amanda. The whole thing's a joke. There is no evil spirit."

"But what if there is?"

"Then we'll *use* it. An evil spirit might help us beat Lincoln Friday night."

Amanda had to smile. "I don't think an evil spirit works that way."

"We'll never know if we don't call it up," Keesha said. "Anyway, Janine wants to make the spirit turn Natalie into a frog or something."

"I bet she does." Amanda laughed. "Okay. I'll tell

Janine to bring the box when we meet at Victoria's tomorrow after practice."

"Great. It'll be fun, you'll see." Keesha paused. "You know, we've really got to do something about Natalie and Janine."

Amanda sighed. "I know."

"Janine is really upset about the way Natalie keeps bad-mouthing Brandon," Keesha went on. "She took it okay for a while. But now it's getting to her."

"You can't really blame her," Amanda pointed out. "I mean, Natalie takes the whole competition between Luke and Brandon way too seriously."

"Yeah, and now Janine's starting to get into it," Keesha agreed. "If the two of them keep fighting, it will wreck all the good feeling on our squad. We'll start messing up our routines and ruin everything." She paused. "Can't you talk to Janine?"

"Why Janine?" Amanda asked. "I was thinking of talking to Natalie. She's the one who started it all."

"I know. But she's not exactly easy to talk to," Keesha replied. "Janine is upset. But she doesn't want this feud the way Natalie does. And Janine is your best friend. She'll listen to you."

And Natalie would probably just get angry, Amanda thought. "Okay," she agreed. "I'll try. Maybe we'll go to a movie tonight and I'll talk to her after."

"No good," Keesha told her. "Janine was on her way out with Brandon when we hung up."

"Oh." Saturday night. And I just broke up with Dustin, Amanda told herself glumly. No date. "What are you doing tonight?" she asked.

"Going out with Andrew, naturally. Got to take a

shower," Keesha added. "See you at practice tomorrow. And remember our plan for tomorrow night—we call up the Evil!"

With a wicked cackle, Keesha hung up.

Amanda gathered all her dirty clothes together, then took them to the laundry room and put them in the washing machine. She took an apple from the bowl on the kitchen table and munched it as she headed back to her room.

Soft music drifted into the hall from the bedroom next to hers. Amanda stopped at the door and poked her head in.

Her older sister, Adele, sat at her desk. One bare foot was propped on it as she carefully brushed her toenails with bright red polish.

Amanda grinned. "I thought you had a research paper to do." Adele's college hadn't started up after the holidays yet.

Adele jumped, painting a red slash across three of her toes. "Amanda! Don't creep up on me like that."

"Sorry." Amanda chomped on the apple. "What about your paper?" she mumbled.

"Finished." Adele grabbed a handful of tissues from a box and wiped her toes.

"How come you're doing your toenails?" Amanda asked. "It's winter. Nobody can see them."

"Because I felt like it."

Adele blew on her nails and lowered her foot. She capped the bottle, then ruffled her fingers through her hair. Like Amanda's, it was a thick, curly auburn, but she wore it short. "How did cheerleading practice go?"

"Fine." Amanda crossed the room and sat on the

bed. As she started to take another bite of the apple, she thought of something. "Hey, Adele. When you went to Shadyside, did you know a cheerleader named Corky Corcoran?"

Adele gasped. Her face turned pale. "Oh, Corky," she murmured. "Oh, poor Corky."

Chapter 6

A SCREAM IN THE GYM

*A*manda stared at her sister, the apple halfway to her mouth. "What happened? Why 'poor' Corky?"

"I . . ." Adele swallowed hard. "I thought I'd finally forgotten. But I guess I'd just pushed it way down in my mind. When you said Corky's name, it all came back."

"What?" Amanda asked. She's going to tell you Corky had some kind of breakdown, she thought.

Adele licked her lips and swallowed again. "What happened was so awful. I had nightmares about it, even though I hardly knew Bobbi."

"Who's Bobbi? I asked about Corky."

"I know." Adele took a shaky breath. "Okay. Bobbi was Corky's sister. She was a year older, but they looked like twins. Blond hair, green eyes. Really great cheerleaders. The best at Shadyside High in years."

Amanda frowned. "I never heard of her."

"Probably because Bobbi wasn't on the squad for long." Adele drew her feet up on the chair and wrapped her arms around her knees. "She died. She was . . . scalded to death."

"Scalded?" Amanda whispered.

Adele nodded. "In the girls' shower room."

Amanda shuddered, remembering Corky's letter. *The Evil killed people in horrible, gruesome ways.*

"How did it happen?" she asked. "Did Bobbi faint and knock herself out or something?"

"No. Somebody—or something—locked the shower doors," Adele said. "No one else was around, and Bobbi couldn't get out. Every single shower head turned on, full blast. And something had clogged the drain. The boiling water kept rising and rising. Bobbi couldn't escape it."

Amanda's stomach churned as she pictured the horrible scene. The big shower room with all those shower heads around the walls. Every one of them on, blasting out water hot enough to burn. And Bobbi Corcoran, trapped inside. Watching the water rise. Feeling her skin begin to blister. Screaming in terror.

"Corky found her," Adele said. "She found her own sister, covered in blisters. Scalded to death."

Corky didn't write about that in her letter, Amanda thought. She probably couldn't stand to think about it.

Her stomach churned again. She tossed the half-eaten apple into the wastepaper basket and swallowed several times. "Did they ever find out how it happened?"

Adele shook her head. "Never. Bobbi wasn't the only one to die, either. And no one could explain

33

those deaths, either. So the rumors got started. Horrible, sick rumors about how an evil spirit had come to life."

Amanda felt the blood drain from her face. The little wooden box with its warning. The papers with instructions on how to call up the Evil. Corky's letter.

Could it all really be true?

"Amanda, are you okay?" Adele asked.

"I'm all right," she lied. "How . . . how did this evil spirit go around killing people?"

"According to the rumors, it possessed the body of one of the cheerleaders," Adele explained. "It killed again and again and the poor possessed girl didn't even know she was doing it."

"Do you really believe this story?" Amanda asked.

"I don't know *what* to believe." Adele rose from the chair and slid her feet into a pair of blue flip-flops. "The whole thing sounds crazy, I know. But people did die. And nobody could ever explain those deaths."

Amanda thought of Corky's letter again. "What about now? I mean, is the spirit supposed to be dead? Or could it be called up again?"

Adele shot her a suspicious glance. "Why are you asking these questions, Amanda? You haven't done anything to disturb the spirit—have you?"

Amanda turned away so Adele wouldn't see her face and know she was lying. "No," she replied. "Of course not."

We haven't done anything to disturb the Evil, Amanda thought as she pulled into the student parking lot at Shadyside High the next afternoon.

We haven't.

And we won't.

She still didn't know whether to believe in the evil spirit. It sounded totally crazy, like something from a horror movie.

But people had died, as Adele said.

Was it just a bunch of horrible accidents? Or had one of the cheerleaders really been possessed?

I don't want to find out, Amanda decided as she climbed out of the car. Why take any chances? Just get that box from Janine and throw it in the garbage.

No—burn it. It will be gone for good that way, joke or not.

Hitching her duffel bag on her shoulder, Amanda hurried across the parking lot. She was late. Not a good example for the captain of the squad to set.

As she pulled open the heavy door, a high-pitched scream echoed down the hallway. It came from the gym.

Amanda frowned and began to run down the hall.

What was going on? Had somebody been hurt?

Another scream pierced the air. The gym doors burst open. Keesha raced out, her face twisted in horror.

"She's killing her!" Keesha shrieked. "She's killing her!"

Chapter 7

EVIL BY CANDLELIGHT

"*H*urry—she's killing her!" Keesha repeated desperately.

"Who?" Amanda called out. "What are you talking about?"

But Keesha spun around and plunged back into the gym.

Another scream rang out as Amanda reached the gym doors. She hurried inside and stumbled to a stop, shocked at what she saw.

At the far end of the gym, Janine straddled Natalie, who lay on her back on the shiny floor. Natalie's heels kicked against the wood and her slender fingers yanked hard at Janine's hair.

It must have hurt, but Janine didn't seem to feel it. Her hands pinned Natalie's shoulders to the floor.

Her round face was red with fury as she squinted down at the other girl.

Keesha darted forward and plucked at the sleeve of Janine's sweatshirt. But Janine ignored her.

Victoria, who was probably strong enough to pull them apart, couldn't seem to move. She stood frozen, watching the fight with a horrified expression on her face.

Amanda flung her bag aside and sprinted toward them.

"You're crazy!" Natalie shrieked up at Janine, trying to twist her body sideways. "Get off me! You're crazy!"

"You're the one who's nuts!" Janine shouted. She lifted her hands from Natalie's shoulders and grabbed her wrists.

Natalie immediately rose up to a sitting position and shoved Janine sideways.

"Stop it!" Amanda shouted, as the two girls tumbled across the floor. Amanda gave Victoria a little shove. "Snap out of it, Vicki! Help me get them apart!"

Victoria blinked, then quickly reached down and wrapped her arms around Natalie's waist. With one jerk, she lifted the slender cheerleader up and dragged her away from Janine.

Janine hopped to her feet and took a step toward Natalie. Amanda and Keesha each grabbed an arm and held her back.

"Cut it out!" Amanda ordered. "Both of you—just stop it!"

Victoria let go of Natalie. Amanda and Keesha dropped Janine's arms.

The two cheerleaders glared at each other, breathing heavily.

"What happened?" Amanda demanded.

"She attacked me!" Natalie declared angrily.

"Because you were laughing at me," Janine shot back. "You are a total jerk, Natalie. Talk about a sore winner!"

Confused, Amanda turned to Keesha and Victoria. "What happened?" she repeated.

"The coach picked Luke to play Friday night," Keesha explained with a sigh. "Brandon will be sitting on the bench."

"And Natalie just couldn't wait to brag to me about it," Janine declared. "As if *she* won the contest, and I lost. Get a life, Natalie," she sneered, her eyes blazing. "Luke is the one who got picked—not you."

Natalie started to reply, but Amanda cut her off. "Don't say anything," she snapped. "Not a single word."

Natalie tossed her dark hair and scowled. But she kept quiet.

Amanda stared at the tops of her sneakers, thinking. I have to do something about this before it gets any worse. I'm the captain. I have to take charge.

Raising her head, Amanda stared at the two angry cheerleaders. "You guys are lucky Miss Daly isn't here today," she told them. "If she had seen this, she'd kick you both off the squad."

"Amanda is right," Keesha agreed.

"This whole competition thing is dumb," Amanda said. "It's not worth ruining everything over."

Silence for a moment. Then Natalie glanced back at Janine. Her gray eyes still looked stormy, but she finally shrugged. "Sorry."

"Yeah. Me too," Janine muttered.

They're still angry, Amanda thought. But at least they're not trying to kill each other. "Okay, time to get to work," she announced. "Let's start with the Hoop cheer."

The cheerleaders quickly arranged themselves in a line and began the cheer.

"HOOP—there it is!
HOOP—there it is!
TWOOOOO points!"

As they worked, Amanda kept glancing at Janine and Natalie. From their grim expressions, she could tell they were just going through the motions. But after a while, they loosened up and began to get into it.

Amanda relaxed a little. The feud is over, she thought. For now, at least.

As they finished the cheer, a door banged open at the other end of the court. The basketball team emerged from the locker room, shrugging into their jackets and swinging duffel bags and backpacks over their shoulders. They had finished practice and were free for the rest of the day.

Brandon walked slowly, head down, shoulders slumped.

Luke strode across the floor with a springy step that made his blond hair bounce. As he spotted Natalie, he shot her a satisfied grin and a thumbs-up.

Amanda glanced quickly at Janine. Janine was tying a shoelace, thank goodness. She didn't see Natalie's gloating expression.

The door banged open again and Judd emerged in

jeans and a dark blue jacket. He paused to zip his backpack. Then he gazed down the court at the cheerleaders.

When he spotted Amanda, he waved to her, a warm smile spreading across his face.

Amanda waved back, feeling her stomach do its funny little flip again.

Whoa, she thought. That was more than just a friendly-type smile. Maybe he really is interested in me.

Amanda turned back to the squad. "Let's do the new routine," she told them. "Miss Daly said it wasn't bad. I want to see if we can actually get a 'good' out of her."

As they moved into position, Amanda caught a glimpse of someone high up in the bleachers. Andrew, she thought, waiting for Keesha.

No, not Andrew, she realized as she glanced up.

Dustin.

Sitting still as a statue, watching her with his green eyes narrowed to slits.

As Amanda stared back, her stomach clenched in a knot and the good feeling about Judd disappeared. Even from this distance, she could feel the cold intensity in Dustin's gaze.

What is he doing up there? she wondered. Why did he stay behind?

And why is he watching me like that?

I hope Janine remembered to bring Corky's box, Amanda thought that night as she walked the two blocks to Victoria's house. I really want to get rid of it. Take it home and burn it in the fireplace.

A gusty wind blew down the street, making the bare

trees creak and moan. Amanda shoved her hands deeper into the pockets of her jacket.

The wind is not even very cold, she told herself. But I'm shivering. Think about something else.

Or some*body* else. Like Judd Hunter.

Picturing Judd's blue eyes and dark hair, Amanda smiled to herself and turned the corner.

In front of her, a tall figure jumped out from the shadow of a tree.

Amanda gasped.

The figure moved closer.

A shaft of moonlight lit up his face. Sandy hair. Green eyes glittering in the light.

Dustin.

"What are you doing here?" Amanda cried. "You scared me to death!"

"Sorry." Dustin came even closer. "I need to talk to you."

"So you decided to hide behind a tree in the dark?" Amanda asked sarcastically.

Dustin frowned. "I wasn't hiding."

You could have fooled me, Amanda thought. She didn't say it, though. The angry look on Dustin's face stopped her. "I have to be at Victoria's," she told him.

"This is much more important," Dustin snapped. "This is about you and me. About what you said yesterday."

"About us breaking up, you mean."

"You never bothered to ask me how I felt about it, you know," he told her bitterly. "Well, guess what? I don't agree with you. I want us to stay together."

Amanda shook her head. "Dustin . . ."

"Hey!" he snapped again. "Don't say no until you think about it. You have one lousy conversation with

41

the golden boy, Judd Hunter, and you decide to break up with me."

"That's not true," Amanda declared.

Dustin sneered. "You think I didn't see the look on your face when you were talking to him? Please. And today when he waved at you, you practically drooled—it was really pathetic."

"Dustin—" Amanda began.

But he interrupted her. "You hardly know the guy, Amanda. What makes you think he's interested in you?"

"Judd doesn't have anything to do with this!" Amanda insisted. "It's you, Dustin. I want to break up with *you.*" She stepped aside and began to walk away.

Dustin grabbed her arm and swung her around to face him. "And what about what I want?" he demanded.

Frightened at the anger and bitterness in his eyes, Amanda wrenched her arm free and ran down the sidewalk.

What's *wrong* with him? she wondered. He's always been intense, but this is different. This is scary.

Still frightened, Amanda glanced back over her shoulder.

Dustin followed her. He wasn't running, but his long legs were quickly eating up the distance between them.

He's crazy, she thought. Crazy!

Putting on a burst of speed, Amanda raced to the middle of the block and up the walk onto Victoria's porch. The front door wasn't locked. Amanda hurried in and locked it behind her.

Breathless, she stood on tiptoe and peeked out the little window at the top of the door.

Dustin stood at the end of the sidewalk. He stared at the house for a few seconds, then jammed his fists into his pockets and walked away.

Sighing with relief, Amanda hurried down the hall to the kitchen. "You'll never believe—" she started.

Then she stopped.

The room was dark except for candles.

Black candles, set in a circle on top of the round oak table.

The other cheerleaders sat around the table, gazing at the flames. The candles waved and flickered, throwing shadows on the walls.

Amanda caught her breath. "What are you doing?"

"You missed it, Amanda," Victoria replied. She smiled, and the candlelight flickered eerily in her eyes. "We called up the evil spirit. It's here!"

Chapter 8

THE EVIL APPEARS

"Huh? No!" Amanda gasped.

"Yes," Victoria insisted. "Can't you feel it? Can't you tell it's here?"

Amanda's knees felt shaky. Her heart pounded. "You shouldn't have done it!"

Keesha laughed. "We didn't."

"Huh?"

"Relax, Amanda," Natalie told her. "Victoria was just joking. We didn't call up any evil spirit."

Amanda sagged against the door frame in relief.

"We're about to call it, though," Victoria said.

Amanda tensed up again.

"We were just waiting for you," Janine explained. She gestured at the black candles, making the flames waver wildly. "How do you like the atmosphere?"

"You shouldn't be playing this game!" Amanda cried.

"It's not a game," Keesha protested. "Tell her, Janine."

"You remember those papers in the bottom of the box?" Janine asked. "Well, they were pages that had been torn out of a book. A really old book, I think, because the paper's real thin and crinkly and rusty colored. Anyway, it gave instructions on how to call up the Evil."

"Right. You sit in a circle," Keesha said. "And you light one black candle for every person there." She pointed to an empty chair with a candle in front of it. "That's yours, Amanda."

"Come on, Amanda." Victoria patted the empty chair between her and Natalie. "Sit down so we can get started."

"No!" Amanda shouted.

The others stared at her, startled.

"You think this whole thing is a joke, but it's not," Amanda told them. "It's really dangerous."

Victoria and Keesha laughed. Janine snickered. Even Natalie smiled. "Come on, Amanda," Keesha said. "You don't really think anything is going to happen, do you? It's just a goof."

"It's not!" Amanda protested sharply. "I asked Adele about Corky Corcoran. And you know what she told me? Everything that Corky wrote really happened! Her sister Bobbi died. Bobbi was scalded to death in the locker-room shower. And she wasn't the only one. Other people died, too. The Evil possessed some of the cheerleaders—took over their minds. And they killed without even knowing it!"

"Well, that won't happen this time," Janine assured her. "Corky's letter told us how to kill the Evil, remember? It has to be drowned."

"See, Amanda?" Keesha grinned. "All we have to do is tie it to a cement block and toss it in the lake."

"This isn't funny," Amanda said. "Don't you get it? If we call the spirit up, it might possess one of us. One of us might start killing!"

"Get a grip, Amanda," Janine told her. "You're practically hysterical."

"I can't help it!" Amanda took a deep breath and forced herself to speak more calmly. "We shouldn't mess around with this."

Keesha rolled her eyes. Natalie and Victoria exchanged a skeptical glance.

"Don't be such a baby," Janine moaned. "It's just for fun—nothing is going to happen."

The others nodded.

"How can you be sure nothing will happen?" Amanda asked.

"Because none of this spirit stuff is for real." Natalie gathered up her dark hair and began twisting it into a long braid. "It's like playing with the Ouija board."

Amanda stared at her. I'm surprised Natalie wants to go along with anything Janine suggested, she thought. But at least they're not fighting.

"Come on, Amanda," Victoria urged. "Sit down."

Amanda gazed at the eager faces in the candlelight. She still didn't like the idea. But if she agreed to do it, and nothing happened, then the others would drop the whole thing.

"Okay," she finally said. "We *try* to call up the

spirit. But then we forget about it. We're supposed to be talking about our halftime routines, remember?"

"Don't worry, we'll do this real fast," Victoria assured her. "What does it say we have to do, Janine?"

"We all hold hands," Janine directed. "And then we say, 'Come forth, spirit. Rise and walk the earth again.'"

Keesha burst out laughing. "If it's that easy, why doesn't everyone in the world do it?"

"There's more to it," Janine replied. "We have to do a bit of chanting."

"How will we know if the spirit is here?" Keesha asked. "I mean, will it talk to us, or what?"

Janine shrugged. "How should I know? Let's just do it and find out. Everybody ready?"

The five cheerleaders placed their hands on the table and gazed into the flickering black candles.

Amanda suddenly felt cold all over. Even for a joke, this was pretty creepy.

Led by Janine, the other four had already begun chanting the words on the old pages. Amanda's mouth felt dry as she joined in.

Finally the chant ended. Silence filled the kitchen.

Amanda's gaze skipped around the shadowy room. She half expected to see some creature lurking in the corner or a ghostlike figure hovering in the air.

Nothing.

No one. No spirit or ghost.

Except for her friends, the kitchen remained empty. And silent. No ghostly voice called out from the shadows.

"Should we try it again?" Victoria whispered.

47

"No way," Amanda replied. She freed her hands. "Once was definitely enough."

"I guess the evil spirit didn't want to join us," Keesha murmured.

Good, Amanda thought. Let it stay where it belongs.

As she leaned forward to blow out her candle, a blinding flash of white light suddenly split the darkness.

Victoria screamed.

"What *is* that?" Janine cried. "Where is that light coming from?"

The light flashed a second time. Blazing.

Then it went out, leaving the room in darkness again.

"It's suddenly so cold!" Natalie gasped. "Do you feel it? It's *freezing* in here!"

"What is going on?" Victoria cried.

Before anyone could answer, the kitchen door banged open.

A cold wind blew in, snuffing out all but one candle.

In the wavering light, a tall shadow fell across the table.

Then a dark figure slid into the room.

Chapter 9

HE CRUMPLES

Victoria screamed again and leaped to her feet. Her chair tipped over, falling to the floor with a loud crash.

The others sat frozen, staring at the figure looming in the doorway.

Amanda's heart thundered. Her mind told her to get out, but her legs refused to move.

As Victoria scrambled across the room, another figure stepped into the room and flicked on the overhead light.

Everyone stayed silent for a moment, staring in disbelief.

And then Keesha laughed. "Whoa! Do we feel like idiots—or what?"

The others laughed too.

49

Because it was only Judd, standing next to the refrigerator.

And behind him stood Brandon, looking bewildered. "How come it was so dark in here?" he asked.

"I don't believe this!" Victoria cried, sagging against a counter in relief. "It's only you! I've never been so glad to see anyone in my life!"

Keesha blew out the last candle. "So much for the spirit world," she declared. "What are you guys doing here, anyway?"

"We had another practice tonight," Brandon explained. "I was giving Judd a lift. But I decided to stop by and see Janine."

Janine went to Brandon and slipped her arm around his waist.

Amanda turned from them. She stared at Judd.

Something is wrong with him, she thought.

He stood still, gazing around the room as if he'd suddenly landed in a foreign country.

Amanda smiled at him, but Judd didn't seem to notice. He blinked, his blue eyes baffled. And bright. Almost glowing.

Even though Brandon had shut the door, the room stayed cold. Unnaturally cold. Amanda could feel the strange chill settling into her bones.

Amanda shivered, frightened by the cold and the strange expression in Judd's eyes.

"Hey, Judd, stop standing there like a zombie," Keesha joked. "You're freaking us all out. Sit down and join the party."

Judd blinked again and shook his head, as if he were trying to clear it. Slowly, he raised his hand

and wiped it across his face. His hand shook violently.

"Judd?" Amanda stood up. "What is it? What's wrong?"

With a sudden groan, Judd crumpled to the floor.

Chapter 10

DID SOMETHING EVIL HAPPEN?

"**J**udd!" Amanda knocked her chair back and raced around the table. She dropped to her knees beside Judd and peered into his face.

He's so white! she thought in a panic.

"Water!" Brandon barked out. He knelt next to Judd and tried to raise him to a sitting position. "Bring some water. Hurry!"

Victoria rushed to the cupboard for a glass. The others gathered around as Amanda helped prop Judd against Brandon's knees.

"Is he breathing?" Janine asked anxiously.

Natalie rolled her eyes. "Of course he is. He's not dead. He just fainted."

"Thanks, Dr. Morris," Janine snapped.

"Drop it, you guys," Amanda told them sharply.

Victoria hurried over with a glass of water and held

it to Judd's mouth. Her hand shook so much, the water slopped out and dribbled down Judd's chin and throat.

With a frustrated cry, Victoria held the glass in both hands and raised it to Judd's mouth again.

Judd's lips stayed closed for a second, but finally he sipped some water.

Victoria took the glass away.

Judd groaned softly, and his eyes fluttered open.

Amanda let her breath out in relief.

"Hey, man, what happened?" Brandon asked.

Judd struggled up and sat on his own. "Dehydration, I guess," he explained in an unsteady voice. "I always feel so weak after practice. I sweat so much. I lose so much salt."

Brandon turned to Victoria. "Got any Gatorade? That's the best thing when you're dehydrated."

"I'm not sure." Setting the glass on the table, Victoria hurried to the refrigerator and rummaged through it. "Thank goodness. Almost a full bottle."

Amanda and Brandon helped Judd to his feet and into a chair. Victoria returned with a bottle of orange Gatorade.

Judd drank deeply, his hand still shaking a little. He paused, took a few more sips, then set the bottle down.

"You're looking better. Not so pale." Keesha squeezed his arm. "I think you'll live."

"Yeah." Judd gave her a weak smile. "I'll be okay. Sorry about crashing on your floor."

"Forget it," Victoria told him.

"Actually, it was a very dramatic entrance, Judd," Keesha teased. "Did you ever think of trying out for the drama club?"

Judd shook his head. "I don't think I could do that fall again."

Everyone began chatting, relaxed now that the scare was over.

But is it really over? Amanda wondered.

She stared at Judd. Did he faint because he was dehydrated?

Or did something else happen to him as he walked through that door?

Something evil?

54

Chapter 11

A SURPRISE AT THE GAME

"Tigers on the loose,
Tigers on the prowl,
Better run for cover
When you hear the Tigers growl!"

The gym at Shadyside High vibrated with the sound of hundreds of people stomping their feet in rhythm to the cheer.

Amanda leaped into the air, her legs apart in a spread-eagle. This is so great, she thought excitedly as she landed. The screaming voices. The pounding feet. The thundering boom of the bass drum. There's nothing like it.

She glanced down the line at the other cheerleaders. They were pumped too. She could tell by the sparkle

55

in their eyes and the extra energy they put into the routine.

> *"Tigers on the loose,*
> *Tigers at the door,*
> *Better run for cover*
> *When you hear the Tigers roar!"*

The cheer ended, and the crowd whistled and shouted as the cheerleaders ran back to their bench.

And that was just a practice run, Amanda thought as she pulled her hairbrush from her backpack. Wait until they see the real thing.

It was Friday night, cold and starry, with no snow to keep people at home, so the gym was packed. The game between the Shadyside Tigers and the Lincoln Hornets would begin in about fifteen minutes.

The Lincoln cheerleaders, in green-and-yellow uniforms, began a cheer of their own.

"They look good," Natalie commented as she blotted her face with a towel. "They must have practiced like crazy over the vacation too."

"Yeah, but they're not as good as we are," Keesha declared. She took a comb from her bag and tugged it through her short brown hair.

"Right," Victoria agreed. "Nobody is as good as we are."

Amanda smiled. The squad is in great shape, she thought. They'd practiced every afternoon this week. They still hadn't pried a "good" out of Miss Daly. But Amanda could tell the coach was pleased.

Janine and Natalie weren't speaking, but they

weren't fighting, either. Amanda had tried talking to Janine, but her friend refused to discuss it.

Amanda decided to give it time. Maybe they'd make up on their own. And at least their feud hadn't hurt the squad's performance.

As Amanda tugged the rubber band from her hair and gave it a quick brush, she thought about Judd Hunter. She didn't have any classes with Judd. But he always smiled and waved when he passed her in the hall.

He seemed really happy to see her. But he hadn't asked her out.

Maybe he's been too busy practicing for the game, she thought hopefully.

A loud drumroll broke into Amanda's thoughts. She tossed her hairbrush down and leaped to her feet.

The drumroll continued. The crowd stood. The cheerleaders waved their maroon and white pompoms.

The drumroll stopped. A loud cheer erupted.

The Tigers raced onto the floor and began to warm up at one end of the court. The Hornets, in green and yellow, took the other end.

While the teams warmed up, the cheerleaders returned to their bench. Amanda gathered her hair up into a ponytail again and tied a maroon ribbon around it. As she started to call the squad together for a pep talk, she spotted Brandon.

The wiry redhead sat on the team bench, elbows on his knees, shoulders slumped. Instead of watching his teammates, he stared down at his sneakers.

Amanda sighed in sympathy. Brandon wanted the

starting position so much, she thought. I know how he feels. Helpless. Disappointed. Angry. Exactly the way I felt when I didn't get picked for the swim team in middle school.

She glanced at Janine, who sat beside her. Janine was watching Brandon. Amanda couldn't see her face, but she knew her friend must be feeling bad too.

Amanda leaned close to her. "Don't worry," she assured her over the noise of the crowd. "Brandon will get to play. I know he will. It's not like he's off the team or anything."

Janine slowly turned her head.

She didn't look sad or upset. Her round, friendly face had no expression at all, and her brown eyes seemed to stare right through Amanda.

"I'm not worried," Janine declared in a low voice. "Brandon will play."

She said that as if she knows something no one else does, Amanda thought. Almost as if she can see into the future.

"Brandon will play," Janine repeated.

Amanda kept staring uneasily at her friend. She'd known her since grade school, but she suddenly felt as if Janine had turned into a stranger.

Amanda jumped as a loud buzzer interrupted her thoughts.

The game was about to start.

I'll talk to Janine at halftime, Amanda decided. Or after the game. The cheerleaders rose from the bench to watch the opening jump.

The crowd cheered as the starting players gathered in the center of the court.

Lincoln won the jump.

The Shadyside crowd groaned as the kids from Lincoln High whistled and stomped. The Lincoln cheerleaders spread out on the sidelines and led a cheer.

> *"Hear that buzz?*
> *It's the Hornets!*
> *Feel that sting?*
> *It's the Hornets!"*

Lincoln's center dribbled down the court, stopped, pivoted, and tossed the ball to another player.

The Lincoln player faked a pass, then ducked around a Shadyside guard and raced toward the net.

The Lincoln kids shouted and pumped their fists. Their cheerleaders jumped up and down, waving their pompoms and urging their team on.

The Lincoln player stopped suddenly, his sneakers squeaking loudly on the polished floor. He faked a shot. Then he spun around and quickly passed the ball, aiming for a teammate who stood closer to the basket.

The Lincoln player and Luke both leaped high, stretching their arms and reaching for the ball.

Luke snatched it out of the air.

"Yes!" Natalie shrieked. "Go, Luke!"

The Shadyside fans rose to their feet, screaming encouragement.

The cheerleaders waved their pompoms and chanted Luke's name. "Luke! Luke! Luke!"

Luke raced down the floor, a look of total concentration on his thin face. Two Lincoln players cut in front of him, but Luke dodged them easily. More

Lincoln players swarmed ahead of him, but Luke weaved his way through them like a fish darting through water.

"He's going to make it!" Natalie shouted. "He's going to score the first basket!"

The crowd shouted as Luke bulled his way past the last Lincoln player.

The court belonged to him now.

Everyone went wild as Luke raced down the floor, straight for the basket.

"Luke! Luke! Luke!" the cheerleaders chanted. "Go, Tigers!"

Ten feet from the basket now, Luke didn't slow down. Five feet. Three feet.

Luke didn't stop. The ball fell from his hands and rolled to the sidelines. He still didn't stop.

The cheering tapered off. Puzzled murmurs filled the gym.

"What's he doing?" someone shouted loudly. "Is he nuts or something?"

Luke suddenly cut to the right, straight toward the bleachers.

In a blur of maroon and white, he raced across the floor. Amanda saw him coming and tried to grab him.

But Luke swept past her, faster and faster, hurling himself into the bleachers.

People screamed. Others cried out in surprise.

Luke charged up a few steps. Then he stumbled and fell. He slammed against the edge of the bleacher seat, then bounced to the floor.

He landed at Amanda's feet with a thud.

People stared in shocked silence.

Luke didn't move.

"Nooo!" Natalie's scream split the air. She took off down the court, shouting her boyfriend's name. "Luke!"

Amanda stared down at Luke, stunned. What's wrong with his head? Why is it so bloody? And what is that *thing* lying next to him?

She dropped to her knees and froze in horror. The "thing" was the top of Luke's head. His skull. His hair. His scalp—completely torn off.

PART TWO

PART TWO

Chapter 12

WHY DID HE GO BERSERK?

"I still can't believe it," Victoria murmured. She stood in Amanda's kitchen, a sad, confused expression on her face. "It's so unreal."

"I know." Amanda's hand shook as she poured some crackers into a wooden bowl. Nobody can believe it, she thought. But it's true.

Luke is dead.

Four days had passed since the strange, frightening scene in the gym on Friday. Luke's funeral had been held this morning. The casket remained closed. No one was allowed to see him.

I didn't need to, Amanda thought. I'll never forget.

She shuddered, remembering the sight of his face. The top of his head ripped off. His scalp—lying on the floor next to him.

How had it happened? How could his head have hit the bleacher that hard? Hard enough to break through the bone of his skull?

Stop it, she told herself. Stop thinking about it.

Giving herself a mental shake, Amanda picked up the bowl of crackers. "Bring some napkins, would you?" she asked.

Victoria grabbed a handful of napkins from the kitchen table, then followed Amanda through the door into the family room.

Natalie sat stiffly on the stone hearth of the fireplace, gazing into the flames. Her gray eyes were rimmed with red from crying, but they were dry now.

Dry and bitter, Amanda thought.

Janine had curled up on one end of the couch. Brandon sat close to her, his arm around her shoulders. Janine's eyes were pink, too, and she kept glancing at Natalie. She started to say something, then bit her lip nervously.

Keesha sat cross-legged in front of the coffee table, restlessly plucking at the rug with her fingers. She smiled as Amanda and Victoria entered the room. But the smile was forced.

Amanda put the crackers on the coffee table next to a platter of cheese and sat on the other end of the couch. Victoria sighed and sank into one of the overstuffed easy chairs.

No one touched the food.

Amanda cleared her throat. "I know we're all still shocked," she murmured. "Nobody can think of what to say, huh?"

"Luke is dead," Natalie stated in a flat, hollow voice. "Why talk? There's nothing *to* say."

"Yes there is." Janine straightened up and took a

deep breath. "There is something to say—I'm sorry, Natalie. I'm so sorry."

Natalie didn't respond.

"Why are you apologizing?" Brandon asked Janine. "What happened wasn't your fault."

"That's not what I meant," she told him. "I meant that Natalie and I—we used to be good friends. But when you and Luke were competing, we started to compete, too. It got kind of ugly, you know? And I feel terrible about it. It seems so silly now, after what happened. So totally unimportant."

"Yeah." Brandon squeezed her shoulder sympathetically.

Janine gazed at Natalie. "So I want to apologize, Natalie. I'm sorry."

Natalie remained silent for a moment. Then she whipped her head around and glared at Janine. "Do you really expect me to believe that?" she demanded in a bitter tone. "Luke is dead and Brandon gets his position on the team. You're not sorry at all!"

"Natalie!" Victoria gasped.

"Oh, don't look at me like that!" Natalie snapped. "At least I'm being honest. Janine is the one who's lying. She's not sorry. She just said it to make herself look good. She couldn't be happier."

"Come on, Natalie . . ." Keesha started to protest.

"No!" Natalie shot to her feet. "Don't ask *me* to apologize. Everything I said is true, and you know it."

Grabbing her jacket from the hearth, Natalie stormed out of the room.

"Whoa," Keesha murmured.

Amanda glanced at Janine, feeling terrible for her. But instead of looking upset or sad, Janine's face was pinched with fury.

Brandon stood up and hurried across the room. "Let me talk to Natalie," he called back over his shoulder. "Maybe I can calm her down."

"I don't see how he can calm her down," Keesha declared after Brandon left. "After all, Natalie is furious at him too. You heard what she said."

"Janine, are you okay?" Amanda asked.

The anger left Janine's eyes. She tucked her hair behind her ears and nodded. "I'm all right."

"Natalie didn't mean it," Victoria assured her. "She's just upset."

"Right. We can't blame her." Keesha reached for a cracker and bit off a corner. "I mean, Luke is dead. And it was so gross," she added with a shudder.

"The way he ran berserk down the court," Victoria added. "It's like he went crazy. Like he was possessed." She gasped. "What if he was? What if we released the evil and . . ."

"Don't start," Keesha interrupted. "That's a dumb superstition. I don't believe any of it. Luke had a terrible accident. It was just a coincidence, that's all."

"What do you think, Amanda?" Victoria asked.

Amanda didn't know *what* to think. Luke *did* run as if he was possessed. Could Victoria be right?

"Listen," Keesha went on. "Crazy talk about evil spirits isn't going to help us. You don't call up evil spirits in this day and age. Do you really think you can light a few candles, and a few seconds later an evil spirit will come ringing the doorbell?"

As Keesha finished speaking, the doorbell rang.

Chapter 13

JUDD FEELS SO STRANGE

*E*veryone jumped, startled.

Then Keesha giggled nervously. "Talk about coincidence!"

That's all it is, Amanda told herself as she left the room. Pure coincidence. It *has* to be!

The doorbell rang a second time.

As Amanda walked down the hall, she kept trying to convince herself that Keesha was right. There was no evil spirit.

Amanda peered quickly through the fan-shaped window, then yanked open the front door. "Judd!"

"Hi, Amanda." Judd raked his fingers through his black hair and smiled. "I was looking for Brandon."

"Oh. He left a few minutes ago," she told him. "I'm not exactly sure where he went."

"That's okay, I'll catch him later."

Amanda gazed at him a moment. His handsome face was lined with sadness. "Hey, why don't you come in?" she asked. "Some of the squad is here. We're not exactly great company, but . . ."

"It helps to stick together," Judd finished for her.

"Right." Amanda decided not to tell him about Natalie and Janine. She pulled the door open wide. "Come on in."

Back in the family room, Judd unzipped his dark blue jacket and tossed it over the back of a chair. "How's everyone doing?" he asked the others as he sat down.

"Still kind of in shock," Victoria told him. "What about you?"

"I feel the same way." Judd glanced around the room. "Natalie's not here? I wanted to tell her something. Brandon, too. Well, all of you, actually."

"What?" Keesha asked.

"Coach Davis called me up a little while ago," Judd replied. "He and the principal decided we're going ahead with the Waynesbridge game this Friday."

Victoria's eyes widened. "So soon after Luke . . . ?"

"It's in Luke's honor," Judd told her. "We'll dedicate the game to him."

"I think that's a good idea." Amanda hadn't known Luke very well. But she figured he probably wouldn't want the team to fall apart. "What about Natalie?" she asked Victoria. "How will she feel about it?"

"She'll hate it." Janine sighed. "She'll hate seeing Brandon playing in Luke's place."

"I'll talk to her," Victoria said. "I think it's a good idea too."

"Me too. It'll be even better if Shadyside wins," Keesha added. "Waynesbridge is tough."

"The Tigers will win," Victoria declared. "I just know it. Right, Judd?"

"Huh?" Judd had been gazing into the fire, Amanda noticed. Not really listening.

"I said the Tigers will win," Victoria repeated.

"Oh. Sure. Definitely." Judd turned back to the fire.

Sighing again, Janine rose from the couch. "I'm going home," she announced. "I have the feeling that Brandon isn't coming back."

Keesha glanced at her watch and leaped to her feet. "Wow, is it that late? I'm supposed to meet Andrew at the mall in fifteen minutes."

Victoria decided to leave, too. Amanda walked them to the front door, then went back to the family room.

Judd stood in front of the fireplace now, his back to her. He turned when he heard her enter.

He looks so lost, Amanda thought, staring at him. "Are you okay?" she asked.

"I don't know, Amanda," he admitted. "Ever since Luke died, I've been feeling so strange. So mixed-up."

"I guess we all have," Amanda murmured. "What happened was horrible."

"Yes, but that's not what I meant." Judd's hand trembled as he ran it through his dark hair. "I . . . I just don't understand what's happening!"

He's really upset, Amanda thought. She quickly crossed the room and stood in front of him. "What do you mean?" she asked anxiously. "Do you want to talk about it? Maybe I can help."

Almost before Amanda finished speaking, Judd

71

grabbed her shoulders, pulled her close, and kissed her on the lips.

Whoa, Amanda thought. She'd imagined kissing Judd lots of times, but never like this.

This didn't feel right.

Amanda broke the kiss and tried to pull her head back.

But Judd hung on to her tightly, one hand around her waist now, the other one cupping the back of her neck.

Like he's hanging on for his life, Amanda thought. Like he'll drown if he lets go.

What's going on?

"Judd." Amanda worked her hands up to his shoulders and gently pushed him away. "What's the matter? Please tell me."

"I . . . I don't . . ." Judd stammered. He took a shaky breath. "I don't know. Friday, when Luke died, I stared down at his face, and I suddenly felt as if I wasn't me. As if I was standing outside myself, staring down at him."

An icy chill snaked its way up Amanda's spine. Just like the other night at Victoria's house when we were calling up the spirit. Judd walked in . . . and he didn't look like himself then, either.

Amanda sighed, remembering that night. We had just finished calling up the evil spirit. And then there was that sudden, blinding flash of light.

Where had it come from?

It flashed again, brighter than lightning.

Then the room grew cold. So cold.

And then Judd walked in and fell to the floor.

But I saw his face before he collapsed. I saw his

72

eyes. His expression. Distant, as if he were looking through me. Not himself.

Just the way Corky described it. The way she described her friends when they were possessed by the Evil.

Exactly the way Judd is now.

Is *he* possessed?

Is it possible?

"What are you thinking, Amanda?" Judd asked.

She jumped, startled.

"Forget what I said," Judd told her. "I didn't mean to get you upset."

Judd reached out, ready to kiss her again, but Amanda stepped away. "Sorry," she told him quickly. "I just remembered—Mom asked me to start dinner. She and Dad will be home from work soon and I forgot all about it."

Chattering nervously about what a lousy cook she was, Amanda walked Judd down the hall and said good-bye.

As she shut the door and leaned against it, she felt the chill run up her spine again.

I'm afraid of him, she thought, crossing her arms. I'm actually afraid of Judd.

But she couldn't help it. She couldn't stop thinking about Corky's letter. And when she remembered that night at Victoria's house, she couldn't help wondering.

Did we really call up the Evil?

73

Chapter 14

CRACK, CRACK

*A*manda glanced around the gym and felt her heart sink.

Friday afternoon, she thought. A pep rally. School had ended more than an hour before. Everybody should be excited and happy. Ready to rock!

But instead of swarming over the bleachers, laughing and shouting greetings to one another, the kids sat quietly, with gloomy expressions on their faces.

"Everybody is so bummed," Amanda commented to Miss Daly. "No one can stop thinking about Luke."

"That's exactly why we need this pep rally," the cheerleading coach replied. "It won't make us forget what happened to Luke, of course. But it will bring us all together, give us something to look forward to."

"We thought this pep rally and the game would be a

good idea," Amanda told her. "But now that it's happening, it feels wrong. The squad doesn't even feel like cheering. How will we ever get the crowd to cheer?"

"You won't. Not with that attitude." Miss Daly clapped a hand on Amanda's shoulder and gave it a squeeze. "You're the captain, Amanda. It's up to you to get your cheerleaders into the spirit. If you do, the crowd will feel it, and their mood will change."

Amanda straightened up and smiled. "You're right."

"Of course I'm right," Miss Daly said. "Now get your squad together and put some pep into them. I don't want to see any droopy, sloppy cheering out there."

Miss Daly loped over to talk to the principal. Amanda glanced over at the rest of the squad. Victoria and Keesha were warming up. Neither one of them looked very peppy. Not even Victoria, who usually had so much spirit.

Natalie sat on the bench behind them, braiding her long dark hair so it wouldn't flop in her eyes.

Natalie looks so worried, Amanda thought. Is she afraid she'll break down and cry or something? Nobody would blame her.

"Okay, guys!" Amanda called out. "Finish warming up so we can talk about the cheers. Where's Janine, anyway?"

"Over there," Keesha told her, pointing toward the team bench. "With Brandon."

Amanda frowned with concern as she walked down the line toward her friend. Janine had been so quiet all week. So depressed she'd even lost her appetite.

Her round face looked almost thin now, and her eyes had dark smudges under them.

"Hey, Amanda." Brandon gazed up as Amanda sat down next to Janine. "I've been trying to cheer Janine up," he said. "Told every joke I could think of. Can't get a single laugh out of her."

"You must be losing your touch," Amanda replied.

"Never!" he cried dramatically.

Amanda nudged her friend. "You'd better cheer up," she warned. "If you don't, Brandon will put another snake in your bag."

"No way." Brandon cackled. "I already did that. I've got something even better in mind."

Amanda laughed. "Even worse, you mean."

Someone in the band blasted out a sour note on the trumpet, and Amanda stood up. As she did, she spotted Judd, sitting farther down on the bench. He flashed her a thumbs-up.

Amanda gave him a wave, then glanced away. He probably thinks I'm mad at him, she told herself. I wish I could explain, but I can't. How can I tell him I'm afraid he might be possessed by an evil spirit?

She turned back to Janine. "It's almost time. Let's get back to the others. Are you going to be all right?" she asked as they walked toward the squad.

"I don't know. Maybe." Janine stopped walking. "I talked to a counselor," she announced quietly. "About Natalie. I didn't know what else to do. Natalie is so furious with me, I just had to talk to somebody about it."

"What did the counselor say?"

"She told me Natalie would eventually be my friend again," Janine replied. "That it's natural for her to be angry and to blame somebody, and I'm a good target. She said I should give it time."

Amanda nodded. "That makes sense."

"I guess so." Janine sighed. "I just wish I knew how much time. It's really hard having Natalie hate me so much."

"I don't think she really hates you," Amanda declared. "She'll get over this."

Amanda approached the bench where everyone was sitting and gathered them all in a loose huddle. "Okay, guys, let's do this right," she told them. "If we go out there like zombies, we'll be letting the team down. They're playing Waynesbridge tonight in Luke's honor. They want to win, so let's get everybody back in the right spirit. Put everything you have into it."

"Amanda's right," Victoria agreed. "Let's cheer the roof off this place."

Keesha and Janine nodded.

Amanda glanced at Natalie, who still had a worried expression on her face. "Are you going to be okay with this?" she asked sympathetically.

"What? Oh—yes," Natalie replied. "The pep rally is a good idea. But I've been thinking," she added. "And I finally decided—I'm going to tell the principal that we called up an evil spirit. She needs to know."

Victoria gasped. "Why?"

"What does that have to do with anything?" Keesha demanded. "Besides, we didn't really call one up."

"I think we did," Natalie argued. "You saw the way Luke threw himself onto the edge of the bleachers. It was like some weird force made him do it. Something evil."

She really believes we called up the Evil, Amanda thought, staring at Natalie's determined face. Is she right? Did the Evil possess Luke?

Does it possess Judd?

"This whole spirit thing is nuts, Natalie," Keesha declared. "And if you tell Ms. Oakley about it, she'll think *you're* nuts."

"Or she'll start asking all kinds of questions," Victoria added. "We could get in major trouble." .

"I don't care about that," Natalie told her. "And neither should you, Vicki."

Victoria and Keesha kept arguing with her. Amanda didn't know what to think. She glanced at Janine, who hadn't said anything. She just listened carefully, her eyes on Natalie.

"Don't try to talk me out of it anymore," Natalie insisted. "One boy has already died. I think Ms. Oakley should know about it. And I'm going to tell her—right after the pep rally."

A drumroll from the band broke into the conversation. Amanda tried to push the whole thing from her mind. "Okay. Let's go!" she cried. "And remember— give it everything you've got!"

The drumroll ended. The squad ran into the center of the floor and began their first cheer.

> *"Tigers claw, tigers roar,*
> *Tigers run—Tigers SCORE!"*

As the cheerleaders continued, the crowd joined in, but not as loudly as usual. They're about as lively as a bunch of wet noodles, Amanda thought.

Doing back walkovers toward the bleachers, the

cheerleaders picked up their pompoms, then raced to the center of the floor and continued the cheer.

The chanting grew a little louder.

When the cheer ended, the band struck up a march, the kind that usually got the crowd into a foot-stomping frenzy. Amanda kept the squad out on the floor, where they marched in time to the beat and urged the crowd to join in.

The gym roof didn't exactly blow off, but the yelling grew louder and the stomping feet shook the bleachers.

We're doing it, Amanda thought. They're coming alive.

The band finished and the cheerleaders ran back to their bench. Miss Daly clapped Amanda on the shoulder again. "Good job."

Amanda grinned. Finally, she thought. We finally got a "good" out of her.

The new principal, Ms. Oakley, a short woman with iron-gray hair, stepped onto a low platform at one end of the court and blew into the microphone.

"As everyone knows, the Tigers lost a teammate last week," she began quietly. "Of course, Luke Stone was more than a basketball player. He was a son. A friend. A student. Someone we all cared about."

Amanda glanced over at Natalie and saw Victoria put an arm around her shoulders. Natalie sat stiffly, with her eyes squeezed shut.

"Still, Luke loved basketball," the principal continued. "Being a Tiger was an important part of his life. And that's why we decided to honor him by dedicating tonight's game to him. We know the Tigers will play their best, but they need our support. Let's give it to them, the way Luke would have wanted."

The principal stepped down and everyone clapped. Another drumroll sounded and the cheerleaders ran out to begin their second routine.

"Okay everybody, let's do it!" Amanda cried. "Let's make it perfect!"

> *"Tigers on the loose,*
> *Tigers on the prowl,*
> *You better run for cover*
> *When you hear the Tigers growl!"*

In perfect formation, the cheerleaders did back handsprings, landed on their feet, and cartwheeled forward.

The routine ended with all the cheerleaders in splits, arms high above their heads. Breathless, Amanda smiled up at the crowd. It went great, she thought. Better than ever.

Then she noticed the silence. No clapping or cheering. No whistling.

What's going on?

Suddenly, screams of horror echoed through the huge gym.

Amanda hopped to her feet, confused and frightened. What was happening?

Amanda gazed up at the stands. Kids were on their feet, shrieking, pointing down at the cheerleaders.

Amanda turned quickly to the rest of the squad. All of them were on their feet.

All except Natalie.

Natalie sat where she'd landed, in a split.

"Natalie—?" Amanda cried. Then she gasped.

Over the cries of the crowd, Amanda heard a loud *crack, crack.*

Natalie's arms flew up above her head—and snapped back.

Her elbows—Amanda realized to her horror—her elbows were bending the wrong way!

And then with two more loud *cracks*, Natalie's arms broke off and dropped to the floor.

"Ohhh!" people moaned and cried out.

Amanda uttered a sickened cry—as Natalie's face split apart. The skin opened and her skull began to crack.

Crack . . . Crack . . .
Crack. . . .

Chapter 15

THE NEXT VICTIM

Such an eerie silence.

Everyone gaped, sick with horror as a bright red lake of blood pooled around Natalie.

Then the screaming broke out again. A white-faced Ms. Oakley shouted into the microphone, ordering everyone to stay calm and file out through the far doors.

No one paid attention. Screams drowned out the principal's voice as the kids began scrambling down from the bleachers. Gagging and crying, they stampeded across the floor in every direction, desperate to get out of the gym.

Amanda wanted to run, too, but she couldn't make herself move. She stood frozen with shock as the hysterical crowd swarmed around her.

"Amanda!" Victoria shrieked. She clamped her

hands on Amanda's shoulders and clung to her. Tears ran down her face and her teeth chattered so hard she could barely speak. "First Luke and now poor Natalie. It's so horrible! What is going on?"

"I don't know." Amanda put her arms around the taller cheerleader and began walking her toward one of the doors. "Come on, Vicki, let's go home. We can't . . ." She paused, swallowing hard. ". . . We can't help Natalie now."

Victoria sobbed as she and Amanda pushed their way through the hysterical crowd. Out of the corner of her eye, Amanda spotted Keesha.

The tiny cheerleader sat slumped on one of the benches, her eyes squeezed shut. Her shoulders shook as she cried. Andrew sat beside her, holding her tightly.

The rest of the basketball team had scattered, lost in the churning, hysterical mass of people struggling to get out.

When Amanda and Victoria had pushed halfway across the floor, Amanda caught sight of Janine. She stopped suddenly, confused and frightened by the expression on her best friend's face.

Janine stood still, staring at the spot where Natalie lay. The crowd surged around her, bumping and shoving, but Janine didn't move.

The look in her eyes gave Amanda a chill. No tears. No terror.

She seems so calm, Amanda thought.

Almost cold.

How can Janine look like that? Is she in shock?

Or is it something else?

"Why are you stopping?" Victoria cried. "We'll be trampled if we don't keep going."

"You go ahead," Amanda told her.

"But . . ."

"Go on, Vicki." Amanda gave her a little push. "I'll be out soon."

As Victoria let the rush of people carry her away, Amanda turned back to Janine.

Janine hadn't moved.

Coach Davis fought his way through the crowd and covered Natalie with a large piece of canvas.

Janine watched, still perfectly calm.

She has to be in shock, Amanda told herself. That's what it is. She's just in shock because of Natalie's death. Not everyone cries and screams when something terrible happens. Everybody reacts differently.

But as she gazed at her friend, she couldn't stop the frightening thoughts that swirled through her mind.

Luke got the starting position. Then he died.

And Brandon took his place.

Natalie threatened to tell the principal about calling up the evil spirit.

Now she was dead. Her skull cracked in half while the whole school looked on.

Before she could talk to the principal.

Amanda's pulse pounded in her ears as she stared at Janine.

Both deaths helped her, she realized. And there was no way Janine could have killed Luke and Natalie— they both died too horribly.

But an evil spirit could have killed them. An evil spirit living inside Janine's body.

Could this be true? Amanda wondered. Is the Evil inside Janine, not Judd?

Amanda felt herself begin to shake. Did we really

call up the Evil? If we did, is it just going to keep killing and killing?

And who will be next?

I don't know for sure if the Evil is really here, Amanda reminded herself. I can't just accuse Janine of being possessed. Not yet. I have to find out if it's true.

But how do I find out?

And what if it *is* true?

As if she suddenly felt Amanda's eyes on her, Janine turned and stared at her.

Amanda's mouth went dry. Her heart raced even faster. Why is she looking at me like that?

Does she know what I've been thinking? Am I the next one to die?

Eyeing Amanda steadily, Janine began to walk toward her.

The crowd had thinned some, but the gym still hadn't emptied. Ignoring the kids who nudged and bumped her, Janine kept coming toward Amanda.

Amanda couldn't make herself move.

Am I next? she wondered.

Am I next?

Chapter 16

BIG SURPRISE IN THE CEMETERY

"Come on." Without waiting for Amanda to say anything, Janine pulled her toward the locker-room doors.

As they left the gym and entered the quiet, empty locker room, an image of Bobbi Corcoran flashed into Amanda's mind.

Scalded. Blistered.

Dead on the shower-room floor.

Amanda eyed the shower door warily, then snapped her attention back to Janine.

Janine paced the narrow passage between the bench and the lockers, clenching and unclenching her fists.

She's my best friend, Amanda told herself. She won't hurt me.

But what if the Evil is inside her?

Janine finally stopped pacing and spun around to face Amanda.

Amanda stayed close to the door, ready to run if she had to. "What is it?" she asked. "Why did you drag me in here?"

"The Evil," Janine announced.

Amanda licked her dry lips. "What . . . what about it?"

"I read Corky Corcoran's letter again," Janine went on. "And I'm scared, Amanda. Scared stiff!"

Was that the expression on her face before? Amanda wondered. Fear? Fear so strong she couldn't scream or cry?

"I know we were just kidding around when we called up the Evil. But what if it worked?" Janine asked. "Corky said her friends died in horrible ways—just like Luke and Natalie. Maybe we brought the Evil back!"

Amanda sagged against the wall, feeling relieved. Janine wouldn't talk like this if the Evil possessed her, would she? "I've been wondering the same thing," she admitted.

"You have? Thank goodness!" Janine closed her eyes and sighed in relief. "I was afraid to tell anyone. Afraid they'd think I'm crazy."

"Then we're both crazy," Amanda told her. "Because I can't stop thinking about it."

"Me either!" Janine cried. "When Luke died, I tried to tell myself it was just a horrible accident. Like maybe his brain went haywire or something and he couldn't stop himself from running straight into the bleachers."

"But you don't think so anymore?"

Janine shook her head. "I'm not sure. But I kept thinking about Corky's letter. And the Evil. And after what just happened to Natalie, I'm terrified. What if the Evil *did* come back—and it's inside one of us?"

Amanda shivered and wrapped her arms around herself. "What if it's true?" she whispered, almost afraid to say it any louder. "What could we do?"

"Corky's letter," Janine declared. "It said the only way to kill the Evil is to drown it, remember? The possessed person must drown for the Evil to die!"

We don't know who is possessed, Amanda thought. And even if we did, could we really drown someone?

"I'm scared, Amanda," Janine repeated. "I'm so scared."

Amanda clutched her arms and forced herself to stop shaking. "We can't get hysterical yet," she said. "We aren't sure about anything. First we need to know if we really brought back the Evil."

"How?"

Amanda thought a second. "Remember what Corky wrote about that bus that crashed? And that girl—Jennifer—who fell onto Sarah Fear's grave?" Amanda asked. "I think we need to go there, to the Fear Street Cemetery."

Janine's eyes widened. "That creepy place? Why?"

"That's where it all started," Amanda replied. "Corky said the Evil came from Sarah Fear's grave. We have to go there. We have to see if the grave has been disturbed."

Janine nodded reluctantly. "You're right. When should we do it?"

"Now," Amanda declared. "Let's go now, before we chicken out."

Amanda quickly changed out of her uniform, then

grabbed her jacket, and hurried out of the locker room with Janine.

The gym had emptied out now. Natalie's body was gone. Amanda glanced at the spot where it had fallen.

The wood was stained a rusty brown color. Stained with blood, Amanda thought.

She glanced away and followed Janine to her car in the student parking lot. They passed a few police officers who were on their way into the school.

"It's starting to get dark," Janine murmured as she drove down Park Drive. "Are you sure you want to do this now?"

"No," Amanda admitted. "But if we wait, I might never do it. Let's get it over with."

"Right." Janine turned onto Fear Street and drove several blocks until she reached the Fear Street Cemetery.

Amanda took the flashlight from the glove compartment and climbed out of the car. She turned on the light and gazed over the low stone wall into the graveyard.

Away from the street, up on a hill, were the neat, even rows of tombstones in the new section of the cemetery. In the spring and summer, the grass would be green and clipped, Amanda thought. Flower beds would bloom with color.

She shifted her gaze lower, to the old section. The crumbling gravestones tilted and sagged, as if the earth were trying to drag them down. Weeds and brambles grew wild. Branches torn from trees lay scattered across the graves like dark, twisted bones.

A cold wind gusted down the street. Amanda pulled up the hood of her sweatshirt. "Come on," she murmured. "Let's do this fast and get out of here."

"Real fast," Janine agreed, her teeth chattering.

Mud mixed with snow had turned the narrow path into a swampy mess. Amanda walked slowly, shining the flashlight beam over the old gravestones. Age and weather had worn the names and dates from some of them.

Amanda's breath steamed in the chilly air as she stepped through the muck under her feet. The wind made her eyes tear. Every time a branch creaked, her heart leaped with fear.

Maybe this wasn't such a great idea, she told herself. I'm cold and I'm scared, and I don't even know what I'm looking for. What can Sarah Fear's grave tell me, anyway?

Behind her, Janine gasped.

Amanda spun around. "What? What?"

"I thought I heard something," Janine whispered. "Listen."

Amanda held her breath. Bare branches creaked in a light wind. Dead leaves rustled as they scattered over the gravestones. Amanda's heartbeat thudded in her chest.

Janine shrugged. "I guess I'm freaked."

"You're not the only one," Amanda admitted. "Five minutes, okay? If we don't find it by then, we'll get out of here."

Janine nodded.

Amanda turned around and walked a few more feet. The flashlight picked out a small grouping of headstones on her right. Four of them were worn so badly she couldn't make out the names.

But she could read the fifth one clearly. SARAH FEAR: 1875–1899.

"Janine!" she called. "I found . . ." She broke off,

staring in shock as the flashlight beam dipped down to the bottom of the stone.

The grave was open!

Mounds of dirt were heaped on either side of it. But not neatly. Not as if it had been dug with shovels.

It's like something burst up from the earth, Amanda thought.

Amanda's hand shook.

The flashlight beam wavered, creating weird shadows. Beside her, Janine gasped. "Look! Look in the grave!"

Clutching the flashlight with both hands, Amanda aimed the beam into the dark, gaping hole.

A wooden coffin lay deep in the muddy earth. Rotting. Worm-eaten.

Open.

And empty.

Chapter 17

A NASTY FALL

*A*manda stared down, terrified. How could this happen? How could the grave be empty? It was impossible, unless . . .

Janine clutched Amanda's arm. "Listen!" she whispered. "Somebody's coming!"

Amanda didn't need to hold her breath to hear the sound. A snapping twig. A soft thump. Another snap.

Footsteps.

Another twig snapped. Another footfall squished on the muddy path.

It can't be true, Amanda thought.

But the grave is open. The coffin is empty.

"It's the Evil!" Janine repeated, tugging frantically at Amanda's arm. "Come on! Run! Run before it gets us!"

Amanda's legs unlocked. She spun away from the

open grave and crashed into Janine, who was still trying to pull her along.

They staggered apart, almost whimpering with fear. Amanda's arm shot up as she tried to keep her balance. The flashlight beam waved wildly over Janine's terrified eyes, the twisted tree branches, the soggy path.

And Dustin's face.

"Dustin!" Amanda cried.

"Huh?" Janine gasped. When she saw Dustin, she sagged against Amanda, shaking all over.

Dustin shaded his eyes against the beam of the flashlight. "You want to take that thing out of my face before I go blind?"

Amanda lowered the light. "What are you doing here?" she demanded. "You scared us to death!"

"I didn't mean to," Dustin protested. He wore his maroon-and-white letter jacket and an old baseball cap over his sandy hair.

Janine straightened up and tucked her tangled hair behind her ears. "What's the matter with you? Why didn't you call out or something?"

"Sorry. I didn't mean to scare you." Dustin stuffed his hands in his pockets and hunched his shoulders against the chill. "What are you two doing here?"

"You first," Amanda insisted. "What did you do— follow us?"

"Sort of," he admitted.

Janine snorted. "How can you 'sort of' follow somebody? Either you did or you didn't."

"Okay, I did." Dustin stepped closer to Amanda. "I have to talk to you," he told her. "I tried to get to you after the pep rally, but the place had gone wild. And then I saw you and Janine leaving, so I came after you. I had to."

"This isn't exactly a good time. Or place," Amanda snapped, taking a step back.

"Don't!" Dustin cried sharply. "Don't run away from me. We have to talk! Now."

Amanda froze, frightened by the intense expression in his eyes. "Please, Dustin. I'm cold and tired and freaked out about Natalie. We can talk later. You can call me."

Dustin shook his head. "Now," he repeated.

"This sounds like a major personal discussion," Janine declared as she started down the path. "I really don't want any part of it."

"No—wait, Janine," Amanda called. "I'm coming with you."

Janine stopped and glanced back, waiting.

Amanda began to step around Dustin.

He quickly moved in front of her, blocking her way.

"Dustin, I want to go home," Amanda told him.

"I'll drive you," he offered. "We'll talk in the car."

"I don't want to talk now!" she cried. "Get out of my way."

Amanda tried to step around him again, but he blocked her path.

"Move!" she shouted angrily. "Dustin, move!" Furious and frightened, she wrenched her arm free and shoved him.

Dustin staggered back.

Amanda began to dart around him. But her left foot slid out from under her.

She struggled to keep her balance, but the soft muck slithered underneath her feet and she began to fall.

Her heels slid over the mud.

She screamed and waved her arms wildly.

But her hands grasped only air.

Screaming again, Amanda toppled back—and plunged straight down into the gaping hole of Sarah Fear's grave.

Chapter 18

GOOD-BYE, AMANDA

*A*manda landed flat on her back with a force that knocked her breath out.

Paralyzed, she squeezed her eyes shut.

A warm current of air flowed around her, making her feel as if she were tucked in bed under a soft comforter.

Not in bed, she told herself in a sudden panic. I'm in a coffin. Sarah Fear's coffin!

Her eyes snapped open. Her breath came rushing back. She gagged at the putrid, rotting smell.

Clumps of muddy earth slipped from the sides of the grave and fell into the coffin. One landed on Amanda's chest, another on her face.

With a scream of terror, she grabbed fistfuls of the stinking dirt and flung it away.

"Amanda!" Dustin peered over the edge of the grave. "Are you all right?"

"Help me up!" she cried, struggling to sit. The soft, moist earth kept spilling down. The putrid muck oozed through her hair and began to slide down her face. "Help me out of here!"

Janine appeared next to Dustin. "Don't panic. We'll get you out," she called down. "Stand up, okay?"

Amanda rose to her knees and braced herself on the edge of the coffin.

With a crunch, the rotting wood gave way under her weight.

Crying out, she fell back. She glanced around in panic. I'm in a coffin! A dead woman's coffin!

"Are you hurt?" Dustin called.

"I . . . I don't think so." Amanda's teeth chattered, even though she could still feel the warm air flowing around her.

Why is it so warm? she wondered.

How can a grave be so warm?

"Come on, Amanda—stand up," Janine urged. She and Dustin stretched their hands down into the grave. "Get on your feet and hold up your arms so we can grab your wrists."

"Okay." Amanda struggled to her knees again. She got one foot underneath her, then the other. Carefully, she rose to a standing position and raised her arms above her head.

Only a few inches separated her fingers from Janine's and Dustin's.

"Stand on your tiptoes!" Janine cried as she and Dustin strained to reach farther into the grave.

Amanda rose to her toes, reaching frantically. Her fingertips brushed Dustin's.

"Almost!" Dustin cried. "Just a little bit more!" He and Janine peered down anxiously, urging her on.

Amanda knew she was getting hysterical, but she couldn't help it. Desperate to get out of the stinking grave, she stretched her arms as high as she could.

Dustin's fingers brushed hers again, then they slipped away. Amanda cried out and tried again.

But Dustin's hands seemed farther away than ever. She couldn't come anywhere close to them.

And then his face began to fade.

Beside him, Janine's face grew smaller and smaller.

"No!" Amanda screamed, reaching up to them. "Don't leave me! What are you doing?"

They didn't answer. Their faces faded. Grew smaller. Farther away.

"Come back!" Amanda begged. "Please! Don't leave me here!"

Their faces grew fainter. Smaller, like pale circles in the darkness.

"Don't leave!" Amanda cried. "Janine! Dustin, please!"

Amanda couldn't even make out their features anymore. They kept fading, farther and farther away—until they disappeared completely.

Amanda gasped. She was falling backward again. She braced herself for the sudden jolt of the coffin at her back.

But nothing stopped her. All she felt was the warm air wrapping her like a blanket as she kept falling and falling.

What is happening? she wondered, screaming in terror. What is happening to me?

PART THREE

PART THREE

Chapter 19

A HUNDRED-YEAR-OLD SECRET

*A*s the warm air swirled around her, Amanda plunged through pitch-black space.

A nightmare, she told herself. That's what it is. I fainted or hit my head and now I'm dreaming. But I'll wake before I land.

In a dream, you always wake before you land.

Amanda closed her eyes against the swirling darkness and waited for the nightmare to end.

After a few seconds, something hard slammed painfully against her back. Her eyes flew open.

Still dark.

But not the pitch-black darkness she'd fallen through.

A ribbon of pale gray clouds sat on the horizon, slowly turning pink as the sun rose behind them. The sky gradually grew lighter, and Amanda could see the outlines of an enormous stone mansion several yards away.

Amanda frowned. There was no mansion in the Fear Street Cemetery. So where was she? How did she get here?

Amanda felt panic creeping into her. What was happening?

A creaking noise made Amanda jump, and she gasped in pain as her back scraped across something rough and hard. She realized she was sitting, leaning against something.

Carefully, she rose to her feet and turned around.

She was standing in front of a small stone house several yards from the big mansion. An oil lamp burned in the window of the small house, throwing a circle of yellow light on the cobblestones.

Near the front door stood an old-fashioned carriage, sort of like a stagecoach, but smaller. A breeze stirred, and the carriage creaked. Two long wooden shafts hung down from the front of it, their ends resting on the cobblestones.

It's where a horse would be hitched up, Amanda thought. An old-fashioned horse-drawn carriage. A mansion. A carriage house. Oil lamps and cobblestones.

What is this place? *Where* is it?

Amanda glanced back at the house. The lamp was out now, and she could hear voices. Women's voices, speaking urgently. The door handle rattled and the voices grew louder.

Amanda ducked behind a carriage wheel and crouched down, her heart pounding.

"I'm so afraid, Sarah," one woman declared in a

high, nervous voice. "What will happen if I'm discovered?"

"You won't be, Jane," a second woman assured her. Her voice was lower, more confident.

Amanda peeked out from behind the wheel. Sarah, the woman who was speaking, had blond hair and a stubborn tilt to her chin. Jane's hair was a flaming red and she had a sprinkling of freckles across her rosy cheeks.

Both women were around twenty. They wore their hair piled high on their heads, with silk ribbons twisted through it. Both wore old-fashioned dresses with pinched-in waists and long skirts.

"It *will* work, Jane," Sarah insisted. "You were so clever to think of it. Don't change your mind now. You want to marry and have children, don't you?"

"Yes," Jane agreed softly. "I want it more than anything. I envy you, Sarah."

"And I envy you!" Sarah told her. "You're going to travel to Europe. I've always dreamed of that. It's so unfair—why should I marry Thomas Fear? I've never even met the man!"

Amanda tensed up. Thomas Fear? Was this woman Sarah Fear?

"But my grandmother arranged the wedding," Sarah continued bitterly.

"Yes," Jane agreed. "And she'll be angry if you don't do as she wishes."

"Not as angry as I am." Sarah paced a few steps, her long skirt swishing on the stones. She clenched her fists and her green eyes glittered with fury. "I hate being told what to do and whom to marry. I won't do it!"

Amanda shivered, frightened and confused. What is going on? Sarah Fear lived a hundred years ago. So how can I be seeing this? How can this be happening?

"And you devised the perfect solution," Sarah said, turning to Jane. "You'll be me—Sarah Burns. You'll travel to Shadyside and marry Thomas Fear. I'll become Jane Hardy and go live in London. We'll both be happy. Isn't that what you want?"

"Of course," Jane agreed. "And yes, it was my idea, Sarah. But now that we are about to change identities, I'm so worried. What if someone in Shadyside finds out?"

"How can they?" Sarah demanded. "Remember, my grandmother is too old to make the trip with me. And no one there knows what I look like. Jane, please. We have to take the carriage to the train soon!"

"I know. But I'm frightened," Jane confessed.

"Think about getting married, having a beautiful wedding and becoming Sarah Fear," Sarah told her. "You'll have a husband and children. You'll live in a big mansion in Shadyside. It will be wonderful."

"And you'll be in London, going to the theater and dining out." Jane's lips suddenly curved in an eager smile. "It *will* be wonderful, won't it?"

"It will be perfect!" Sarah cried excitedly.

Amanda shivered again. The words were finally starting to sink in.

Sarah sailing to Europe in Jane's place. Jane going to Shadyside, pretending to be Sarah. Marrying Thomas Fear.

They're talking about switching places, Amanda realized.

Switching identities!

Jane laughed, her voice high and excited. They seem so real, Amanda thought. I can smell their perfume. I can hear the swish of their skirts. The sound of their high-buttoned boots on the stones. I can feel the carriage wheel digging into my shoulder.

Did I travel back in time?

But that's impossible!

Isn't it?

Sarah clapped her hands, interrupting Amanda's thoughts. "Quickly now, we don't have much time, Jane. We have to hitch up the carriage or we'll miss the train."

They're coming toward me! Amanda realized. What if they can see me? What will they do?

Hide! she told herself.

Amanda stood up, ready to run behind the house as soon as they turned their backs. But her legs were numb from crouching so long and she stumbled, falling hard against the carriage wheel.

With a loud creak, the carriage began to roll forward. Amanda grabbed hold of the wheel. But the carriage kept rolling, the two long shafts scraping noisily along the cobblestones.

Amanda stumbled along beside it for a second, hoping to keep herself hidden. Then her toe caught in one of the uneven stones and she tripped. With a cry, she fell to her knees.

The carriage rolled a few more feet, then stopped.

Slowly, Amanda glanced up.

Sarah and Jane stood on the drive, gazing at her. Jane had turned pale, and her eyes were wide and frightened.

Sarah scowled, her eyebrows forming a V over her nose. She pressed her lips together and put her hands on her hips.

Amanda rose to her feet, her legs trembling.

They see me!

Chapter 20

AMANDA DROWNS

Jane twisted her hands together and laughed. A high-pitched, uneasy laugh.

"What on earth happened?" Sarah demanded. "What made the carriage roll?"

Amanda licked her lips. "I did," she admitted nervously. She glanced down at her muddy jeans and sneakers. "Listen, I know this sounds crazy, but . . ."

"Do you think it was a sign?" Jane asked Sarah. She ignored Amanda completely.

"Of what?" Sarah ignored Amanda, too.

"A sign that we shouldn't go through with our plan," Jane replied.

Sarah scowled at her, annoyed. "Don't be silly."

Both women glanced back at Amanda.

They're not looking *at* me, Amanda realized. They're looking *through* me. They can't see me at all.

Am I dead? A ghost? What is happening?

"It must have been the wind," Sarah declared firmly. "You can't be superstitious, Jane. You have a wedding to go to, and I must sail to Europe. We have to catch that train and begin our new lives!"

In only a few minutes, a big chestnut horse was hitched up to the carriage and the two women climbed aboard. As she watched them drive away, terror gripped Amanda.

I can't stay here! she thought. What will happen to me? Am I stuck in the past forever?

Amanda took off after the carriage, running as fast as she could. She knew they couldn't hear her, but she waved her arms and yelled anyway. "Jane! Sarah! Wait! Let me come with you. Wait!"

Jane and Sarah didn't look back. The carriage moved steadily down a tree-lined drive.

Amanda pushed herself to run faster. Her chest began to ache and she felt a stitch in her side. Keep going, she told herself. I can catch it. It's not going that fast.

Gasping for breath, darkness swept around Amanda.

That's weird, she thought. It's morning. It's sunny. It can't be getting dark.

She blinked hard and shook her head. The darkness grew around her. Thick and inky, it blotted out her side vision until she felt as if she were peering down a long tunnel. At the end was the carriage, rolling along in a patch of sunlight.

The darkness closed in. Amanda felt a warm current of air surround her. The same warmth she'd felt in Sarah's grave.

Ahead of her, the carriage grew dim and hazy. Amanda couldn't hear her feet pounding anymore. Couldn't see the carriage at all now.

What is happening to me?

As the inky darkness swallowed her up, Amanda screamed in panic.

Still surrounded by darkness, Amanda felt the earth pitch and roll underneath her. She tried to keep running, but staggered to the side. The pitching, rolling motion continued. Amanda planted her feet apart and held her arms out to keep from falling.

The warm air retreated. A stiff, cold wind whipped through her hair. Drops of water pelted her face. Amanda licked her lips. The water tasted salty.

A man's voice spoke close to Amanda's ear. "We're in for it now," he declared anxiously.

"In for what?" Amanda asked.

The man didn't reply.

"In for what?" Amanda repeated, raising her voice. "What's wrong? Can't you hear me?"

Still no reply.

A gust of wind plastered her hair across Amanda's eyes. Frustrated, she peeled it away.

With a gasp, she realized that the darkness had lifted and she could see.

She stood on the deck of a large ship, surrounded by women in long dresses and men wearing straw hats and old-fashioned suits. Most of them stood at the railings, staring down in fear at the surging waves below.

The ship rose on a swell of slate-gray water, hung

there for a moment, then plunged into a trough between two waves. Amanda's stomach plunged with it. Cold water swept across the deck, swirling and frothing around her ankles.

Women screamed and hitched up their skirts. Men's hats blew off their heads and spun through the air, disappearing into the chilly mist.

The man standing next to Amanda held on to his hat with one hand and stuck his other arm out for balance. "We're in for it now!" he shouted again. He seemed to be staring at her, but she realized he didn't see her at all.

It's just like before, she thought. I'm invisible to these people.

The ship rose again, climbing the wave slowly, like a roller coaster on the first big hill. Amanda steadied herself for the plunge. But when it came, she couldn't keep her balance. She staggered across the deck and slammed into the railing.

Her stomach churning like the waves, Amanda held on to the slick railing and tried to prepare for the next roller-coaster ride. She felt too sick and cold to worry about where she was or how she'd get out of it.

The next wave came and the ship slammed down. But when it landed this time, it landed at a tilt.

People screamed again, lurching across the sloping deck and crashing into the railing.

"We're capsizing!" someone shouted. "We're going to go down! Get the lifeboats!"

"It's too late!" someone else called out.

"Nooo!" a woman's voice screamed. "It can't be too late. It can't be!"

At the sound of the woman's voice, Amanda turned.

Sarah Burns stood next to her, braced against the railing on the high side of the ship.

She's on her way to London, Amanda realized. Heading across the ocean to a new life as Jane Hardy.

Sarah's hair had come down and blew around her head in wet, tangled strings. Her green eyes flashed with fear and frustration.

"Where's the captain?" she shouted angrily. "What is he doing? Can't he save his own ship?"

"He's trying," a man screamed back. "He can't fight the ocean. It's too strong!"

The ship tilted farther to the side. A wave rose up and crashed to the deck.

Amanda clung to the railing, gasping and terrified.

Beside her, Sarah screamed again. "I'm not supposed to die now! How can this be my fate? I'm supposed to be on my honeymoon with Thomas Fear!"

No one paid any attention to her. Their screams almost drowned out her words as they tried to climb to the high side of the ship, away from the churning ocean.

"Why?" Sarah lifted a fist and shouted to the sky. "Why did I trade places with Jane, only to die in her place?"

Another wave swept over the deck. Men and women struggled to hold on. But the force of the wave washed them into the ocean like rag dolls.

A shudder passed through the ship. It tilted again, until it lay on its side. People fell screaming into the ocean.

Amanda crashed to her knees, clinging to the railing. But she could feel her fingers growing numb. I can't hold on much longer! she thought desperately. Please let this be a nightmare! Please let me wake up now!

The ship began to nose downward. Water rushed over the bow, slamming into Amanda with so much force it knocked her legs sideways. She could see Sarah next to her, struggling to hold on too.

But the ocean was too strong. The next wave pried Amanda's hands from the rail and swept her off the deck.

As the icy water closed over her head, Amanda saw Sarah thrashing next to her, her long skirt tangled around her legs.

"This isn't fair!" Sarah shouted.

But we're underwater, Amanda thought. Her mouth is closed. How can I possibly be hearing her?

"I'm going to die! But this is Jane's fate, not mine!" Sarah's words were clear and loud as she struggled in the churning water.

It's her thoughts, Amanda suddenly realized. I can hear what she's thinking.

"It shouldn't be me!" Sarah screamed again. "It should be Jane who drowns, not me!"

The fear had disappeared from Sarah's voice. All Amanda heard now was anger. It burned in her eyes and twisted her face into a hideous mask of fury.

"It's not fair!" Sarah screamed. "Not fair. Not fair! Not . . ." Her voice suddenly stopped.

She whipped her head back and forth, trying desperately not to breathe.

But her lips parted.

114

Her eyes widened.

Her body thrashed crazily for a few moments. Then it went limp, and a stream of bubbles drifted from her mouth.

Dead, Amanda thought. She floated easily under the water, staring at Sarah's body as the motion of the waves rolled it over and over. She's dead.

Sarah's body rolled again, turning on its back. Her eyes were still open.

And still filled with rage.

A vicious, white-hot rage that Amanda could almost feel.

I *do* feel it! Amanda suddenly realized. Sarah is dead, but I can still feel her anger. It's pouring out of her eyes. It's turning the water hot.

The water began to churn and bubble. Amanda felt its heat sizzle on her skin as it grew hotter and hotter.

It's boiling!

Sarah's anger is so powerful, it's boiling the water.

As the heat grew stronger, Amanda suddenly noticed the smell. A foul, putrid odor that reeked of death.

She stared at Sarah and gasped.

A green, snakelike liquid was pouring from the dead woman's mouth.

Thick and reeking, the horrible stuff kept twisting up from between Sarah's lips like a giant snake.

Amanda shuddered with terror.

It's Sarah's rage. I can feel it inside the green form. Pulsing. Throbbing with life.

With hate.

With revenge.

As the green form kept rising, it reared up like a cobra, hovering over Amanda's head.

And then it began to spread, turning the boiling water green.

Filling the water with its hatred.

Pouring out of Sarah's corpse. Surrounding Amanda with its evil, undying rage.

Evil, Amanda realized in horror.

It's the Evil!

PART FOUR

PART FOUR

Chapter 21

OUT OF THE GRAVE

Amanda opened her eyes to darkness.

Sarah's body no longer floated in front of her. The horrible green liquid that poured from her mouth had disappeared. Amanda couldn't feel Sarah's rage now.

Was the Evil gone?

"Amanda?" an anxious voice called out.

Dustin's voice.

"Come on, get up!" he urged.

"She can't get up!" Janine's voice snapped. "Didn't you see her fall? She must have hit her head and blacked out. Amanda, are you okay?"

The darkness began to fade. The warmth disappeared. Amanda shivered and began to sit up.

Cold water streamed from her hair and ran down her neck. She shivered again and glanced around.

Walls of dirt rose on all sides of her. Moist, smelly earth lay in clumps in the wooden box she sat in.

The box!

Amanda shuddered as the memory came rushing back. I fell into Sarah Fear's grave. I'm sitting in her coffin!

She glanced up. Janine and Dustin hung over the edge of the grave, worried expressions on their faces. "Can you stand?" Janine asked.

"Yes!" Amanda scrambled to her feet, frantic to get out of the grave. Her jeans and sweatshirt were drenched. She felt chilled to the bone.

And the water that trickled over her lips tasted salty.

Ocean water.

It wasn't a dream! she realized with a shudder. I really did go back through time.

I saw the birth of the Evil!

Terrified at the memory, Amanda stood on tiptoe and stretched her arms high above her head. "Please! Get me out of here!"

Her fingertips brushed Janine's, then Dustin's. Finally, Dustin inched himself farther over the lip of the grave and managed to catch hold of her wrist.

As Dustin pulled, Amanda jammed the toes of one sneaker into a muddy wall and rose up a little higher. Janine caught her other wrist. Together, she and Dustin pulled Amanda from the grave of Sarah Fear.

Amanda stumbled out and sank to her knees, panting with relief.

"Are you all right?" Janine asked.

"No." Amanda's teeth chattered. She couldn't stop shaking. "I'm not all right."

"You hit your head, didn't you? I'll take you to the hospital," Janine declared. "You might have a concussion."

"I don't," Amanda insisted. "I didn't hit my head. Something happened to me, but not that."

"Well, what?" Dustin asked.

Amanda caught her breath and stood up. "I traveled back in time."

"Huh?" Janine frowned at her. "Whoa!"

"It really happened!" Amanda insisted. "There's something supernatural about that grave. When I fell into it, something—some force—pulled me back in time. And now I know what happened. I know how the Evil was born."

Dustin raised his eyebrows. "What evil?"

"Sarah Fear's Evil," Amanda replied, pointing to the grave.

Suddenly Amanda realized something. Something horrible. "But this isn't really Sarah's grave. Sarah drowned—she never lived in Shadyside with Thomas Fear. This grave . . . it must be *Jane's* grave."

Janine frowned again. "Amanda, you're babbling."

"Listen to me!" Amanda cried. "When I went back in time, I saw Sarah Fear. Only she wasn't married yet—her name was Sarah Burns. And she never became Sarah Fear. She switched identities with her friend, Jane Hardy."

"Amanda—" Dustin cut in.

"Don't you get it?" Amanda cried. *"Jane* came to Shadyside and married Thomas Fear. She pretended her name was Sarah. But the real Sarah sailed for London. Only she never made it. Her ship went down and she drowned."

121

Janine and Dustin stared at her, astonishment in their eyes. "That's enough, Amanda," Dustin declared. "Stop this crazy talk."

"I'm telling the truth," Amanda insisted. "I was right there. I saw Sarah drown. And she was so furious! It was horrible. Terrifying. Even after she died, the fury just kept pouring out of her. I could actually see it and feel it! She was dead, but it was alive. And it was the Evil!"

"Amanda, you were only in the grave for a few seconds," Janine told her. "You must have blacked out and had some kind of nightmare or something."

"Look at me!" Amanda shouted, grabbing her hair and wringing the water from it. "I'm soaking wet. How do you think I got that way?"

Dustin shrugged. "There's water down in the grave."

"No. I was in the ocean," Amanda insisted. "I saw the Evil being born." She paused, frustrated. They don't believe me. Do they think I'm lying? Or crazy?

She glanced at the grave. "Okay, if you don't believe me about the time travel, look at the grave. It's empty. So is the coffin. How do you explain that?" she demanded. "What happened to this grave?"

Dustin and Janine shrugged.

"Sarah's evil spirit must have gone to Shadyside," Amanda said. "She went after Jane—she was so angry at Jane. And the Evil took over Jane's body and made her kill people." She stared into Janine's eyes. "We called up that Evil. It burst out of this grave."

"I don't know what to think," Janine admitted with a sigh. "This whole thing is really creeping me out. And so is this horrible cemetery. Let's go."

Turning their backs on the empty grave, Janine and

Dustin hurried away. Amanda followed. By the time they reached the street, she was shivering violently. She was soaked to the skin and covered with mud. Mud that reeked of decay and death.

Jane's death. And Sarah's death.

Except Sarah isn't truly dead, Amanda reminded herself. Not as long as the Evil lives.

And it does live.

On the street, Dustin said a quick good-bye and hurried to his car.

"I guess he doesn't want to get back together anymore," Amanda murmured as she climbed into Janine's car. "That's one way to get rid of him—make him think I'm nuts."

Janine didn't reply. She started the car and pulled away from the curb so quickly the tires squealed.

Amanda turned to her. "What about you? I suppose you think I'm nuts too."

"No way," Janine protested. "But this is so weird. I'm totally confused."

"So am I," Amanda admitted. "But I know what I saw. Sarah's Evil was so strong. Too strong to die. And it came back through Jane's grave."

Janine's fingers tightened anxiously on the steering wheel. "But if it really is back, what can we do?"

"I'm not sure. But we have to be careful," Amanda warned. "The Evil is inside someone. We just don't know who."

Janine nodded and bit her lip nervously as she turned the car into Amanda's driveway.

"Don't go all the way to the house," Amanda told her. "If my parents hear the car, they'll come to the door. I don't want them to see me like this. I'll walk up the driveway and sneak in the back."

Janine stopped the car at the foot of the drive. Amanda climbed out. As Janine pulled away, Amanda started toward the house.

And stopped.

A set of footprints led up the drive.

Clumps of thick, moist earth had scattered around each print.

Amanda gasped.

It looks like mud from the grave.

But it doesn't have to be, she told herself. It probably isn't.

Amanda continued up the drive. But she kept one eye on the footprints.

Halfway toward the back, the prints stopped.

Amanda's heart seemed to stop too.

The muddy footprints led straight up to her bedroom window.

Chapter 22

A VISITOR

Amanda backed away from the footprints. Her heart was racing now, and her legs felt shaky.

Something rustled in the hedge behind her. Amanda jumped, then sped down the walk and into the kitchen through the back door.

"Amanda?" her mother's voice called from the front of the house.

Amanda caught her breath and tried to steady her voice. "Yes. It's me."

"We were getting worried. You should have called."

"Sorry." Amanda kicked off her filthy sneakers and picked them up.

"Your father and I are just leaving," her mother told her. "We're having dinner with the Dixons, so you're on your own. There's leftover chicken in the refrigerator."

Amanda's stomach tightened into a knot. After falling into that grave, she couldn't imagine ever eating again.

Her parents called out good-bye, and the front door slammed.

Amanda stood in the kitchen, listening. Her sister Adele had gone back to college yesterday. Silence in the house now. All Amanda heard was the hum of the refrigerator and the steady tick of the hallway clock.

Clutching her sneakers, she left the kitchen and crept down the hall.

She stopped at her bedroom door. As she reached for the handle, terror shot through her. She quickly snatched her hand back.

The footprints! The muddy footprints had led to her bedroom window!

Had someone climbed into her room?

As Amanda stood in the hall, a clump of mud oozed down her jeans and plopped to the floor. Water dripped from her hair. Her fingers and toes felt numb from the cold.

You have to go in, she told herself. You have to get out of these clothes and into something warm and dry.

Amanda forced herself to take hold of the door handle. She sucked in her breath, quickly turned the handle, and pushed the door open.

A wave of air rolled out, its smell so sour that Amanda staggered back a step, dropping her shoes to the floor. She gasped, then almost gagged as the foul smell filled her nose again. Her stomach heaved and tears sprang to her eyes.

"Amanda," a voice whispered from inside the bedroom. "Come in."

Amanda gasped again. The voice sounded hollow. Thin and hollow, as if whoever spoke had no strength.

The thin, whispery voice repeated her name. "Amanda."

Amanda blinked the tears from her eyes and stared through the doorway.

A woman stood in the center of the room.

A dead woman. Half corpse. Half skeleton.

Tattered shreds of rotting flesh dangled from the bones of her shoulders and arms.

Strips of what had once been a long skirt hung like ribbons around her leg bones.

Only a few wisps of hair clung to her skull.

One eye was missing. The other had oozed from its socket and stuck to a jutting, shiny-white cheekbone.

Her nose was a greenish-black pulp of rotting flesh.

One foot was bare.

The other wore a rotting, high-buttoned boot.

Sarah Fear! Amanda thought in horror. It's her corpse!

Run! she told herself. Get out of the house.

But her feet felt rooted to the floor. She couldn't move them. All that moved was her heart, pounding so hard she thought it would burst from her chest.

Sarah raised her arm and crooked a bony finger at Amanda, motioning her inside.

Amanda swayed dizzily.

"Come in, Amanda," Sarah whispered. A decayed chunk of her lip broke off and a stream of rotten breath blew across the room. "We must hurry. You and I are going to trade places now."

Chapter 23

AMANDA DIES NEXT

*A*manda gasped as another wave of dizziness swept over her. The floor seemed to tilt under her feet.

I'm falling, she thought in panic. Falling into the room.

Into death.

The floor tilted farther.

Amanda swayed forward, toward the open door.

"No!" Screaming in terror, she braced her legs and raised her arms to stop herself from falling.

Her hands banged against the door.

She stared at it, blinking in confusion.

The door is still closed, she realized. She ran her palm down the smooth wood.

My bedroom door is closed.

Her knees sagged as relief flooded through her. She leaned her head against the door and breathed deeply.

I imagined it, she thought. That rotting corpse with its sickening smell. That dry, dead voice. I'm still freaked from falling in the grave and going back in time.

I imagined the whole thing.

Amanda closed her eyes and took another deep breath. Then she picked up her shoes and opened the door.

Stepping inside, she quickly flipped on the light.

The room stood empty.

Everything looked the same as it had when she left this morning. Stuffed animals piled on the bed. Books stacked on the desk. A thick, rust-colored sweater and black leggings draped across the chair.

Amanda dropped her shoes and started toward her closet. She needed a long, hot shower and dry clothes.

As she moved farther into the room, she began to unzip her sweatshirt. Mud clogged the zipper and it wouldn't go down. She crossed her arms and grabbed hold of the bottom of the shirt to pull it over her head.

Then she froze, elbows stuck out, heart banging against her chest as she gazed across the room.

The bed had blocked it before, but she now could see it clearly.

A clump of mud, stuck to the windowsill.

More mud beneath the window.

A footprint. Then another and another, leading across her bedroom.

Still frozen in place, Amanda tracked the footprints with her eyes. They led across the pale blue rug, past the closet, and stopped in front of the dresser.

Amanda's eyes traveled slowly up to the top of the dresser.

Her hairbrush. A pair of rolled-up socks. A small

129

plastic tree with earrings and bracelets dangling from its limbs. A bottle of hand lotion.

A sheet of paper anchored beneath the bottle.

Amanda dropped her arms and forced herself to walk toward the dresser. It's only a piece of paper, she told herself. Mom probably left me a note.

But Mom didn't climb in my window and track mud across the rug. And everybody leaves notes on the corkboard in the kitchen.

In front of the dresser, Amanda stopped, gasping. The paper was wet and muddy. But the mud didn't cover the writing, or the bold signature at the bottom:

Sarah Fear.

Amanda's hand shook as she slid the lotion bottle off the paper and read Sarah Fear's message: "You and your friends have awakened a great Evil. The Evil takes pleasure in killing. You are next, Amanda."

"No!" Amanda cried out. She backed away from the dresser, clutching her arms.

First Luke. Then Natalie.

And I'm next, she thought in terror. I'm next!

How will I die? What kind of gruesome "accident" is going to happen to me?

And who will do it? Who is possessed by the Evil? Who do I have to watch out for?

It won't matter, she thought. The Evil is too strong. I saw it. I watched it spew out of Sarah's mouth and boil the ocean.

Even if I find out who it is, I can't fight it. It will get me, no matter what.

Amanda backed up until her legs hit the bed, and she dropped onto it.

Amanda drew her legs up and wrapped her arms around her knees. I can't give up, she told herself.

There has to be something I can do. Some way to stop the horrible Evil before it kills me or anybody else.

Janine, she thought suddenly. Janine has the instructions on how to call up the Evil. Maybe they tell how to get rid of it.

Amanda grabbed the telephone and punched in the number.

Busy.

Amanda hung up and peeled off her filthy clothes. She grabbed her bathrobe from the closet hook and shrugged into it. Then she hurried back to the phone and stabbed out Janine's number again.

Still busy.

I have to talk to her! Amanda thought desperately. I have to tell her what's happened. She'll help me figure everything out.

Go over there, she told herself. Stop wasting time!

She threw off her robe and hurried back to the closet. She dragged out a pair of fresh jeans and pulled them on. She fumbled around for a second pair of sneakers and shoved her feet into them.

Hurry! her mind screamed at her. Hurry!

Racing to the chair, she grabbed up the rust-colored sweater, yanking it over her head as she flew from the room.

In the kitchen, she snatched the car keys from the hook by the refrigerator, then tore down the hall to the front door.

As she turned the handle, a strong gust of cold air blew the door wide open.

Amanda gasped.

Judd stood outside, his face only a foot away from hers.

Amanda stared at him.

"Hi," he said. "Can I come in?"

"I . . . I guess." Amanda backed up a step.

As Judd took a step forward, Amanda heard a squishing noise.

She glanced down.

And gasped again, her heart suddenly racing with fear.

Judd's sneakers were caked with mud.

Chapter 24

BACK TO THE GRAVE

Judd's eyes followed Amanda's gaze to his sneakers. "Looks like I walked through a swamp, huh?"

Or a grave, Amanda thought. "What are you doing here?"

"I stopped by to see how you are," he explained. "I mean, everyone is so scared and upset about Natalie. And I didn't get a chance to talk to you this afternoon. I wanted to make sure you're all right."

Amanda kept staring at him. He's the one, she thought, her heart racing. He must be. He left the note and the muddy footprints in my room. He signed the note with Sarah's name.

The Evil is inside Judd.

Judd shifted his weight, an uneasy expression on his face. "What's wrong?"

"Huh? Oh. Well, it's like you said—I'm upset."

133

Amanda heard her voice shaking and took a deep breath. "But I'll be okay. Thanks for stopping by." She reached for the door and began to swing it shut.

"Hey, wait a sec, Amanda," Judd protested. "I'm kind of freaked about all this. I thought we could talk a little. Can I come in?"

"No."

Judd stared, his blue eyes startled. "I thought you said I could."

Stay calm, Amanda told herself. Don't let him know I'm on to him. "Sorry, I forgot. I was just leaving for Janine's," she explained.

"I'll drive you," he offered.

"No, you don't have to do that. Really," Amanda told him. "It's getting kind of late. I don't know how long I'll be there. Janine's *really* upset about everything, and I don't think she . . ."

"I'll drive you," Judd repeated firmly. "You're really pale, Amanda. You look like you're going to pass out. You can't drive like that."

If she slammed the door in his face, he'd find a way in. If she got in the car with him, she might never reach Janine's.

"Come on." Judd reached out and took hold of Amanda's arm, pulling her through the door. "Let's go."

Feeling helpless and terrified, Amanda walked with him across the porch and down to his car. He kept an arm around her the whole time.

A week ago I dreamed of getting together with Judd, she thought. Now here I am with his arm around me.

But it's a nightmare, not a dream.

As Judd pulled away from the house, Amanda

slipped her fingers around the door handle and pulled.

Nothing happened.

Automatic lock, Amanda realized. Why did I ever get in? Now I'm trapped. Trapped in this car with the Evil.

She glanced at Judd.

His long fingers gripped the steering wheel firmly as he guided the car around a corner. In the glow of a streetlight, his expression seemed calm.

Of course he's calm! Amanda's mind screamed at her. He's in control. You got into the car with him, and now he can kill you anytime he wants!

Feeling her eyes on him, Judd turned his head and smiled.

Amanda smiled back weakly. Sliding her hands up inside the sleeves of her sweater, she huddled against the passenger door.

He's waiting until we get to Janine's, she thought frantically. He's going to kill us both at the same time. He'll burn the house around us. Or blow it up. Something horrible and gruesome.

Amanda shuddered, and Judd glanced at her again. "There's an extra jacket in the backseat," he told her. "Sorry—I didn't give you a chance to get yours before we left."

Before you dragged me out of the house, you mean. "I'm not really cold," Amanda murmured.

Judd turned the car onto Canyon Drive. Amanda tensed up even more. She could see Janine's white, two-story house at the end of the block. Almost there.

Almost dead.

"Isn't that Janine's car?" Judd asked. He pointed at a blue compact backing out of the driveway.

Amanda nodded. She could see Janine's face as she backed the car into the street. Then, as the car turned the corner, she caught a glimpse of Brandon's red hair glowing in the streetlight.

"I thought she was waiting for you," Judd said. "You must have mixed up the time. They're probably going for pizza or something. Want to follow them?"

"I guess," Amanda agreed. If she made it to the pizza place alive, she could jump out of the car and scream for help.

Janine drove quickly through the winding neighborhood streets, then turned down Park Drive. When she reached Division Street, she didn't turn off. Instead, she kept driving to the Old Mill Road, then made a right turn onto Fear Street.

"Guess I was wrong about the pizza," Judd commented. "I wonder where they're going."

Amanda didn't reply. The blue car had pulled over to the curb, and she saw Janine and Brandon climb out.

Another car shot in front of Judd, and he had to stop quickly. By the time he'd started rolling again, Janine and Brandon were out of sight. But Amanda knew where they had gone.

Into the Fear Street Cemetery.

What is going on? she wondered as Judd pulled to a stop behind Janine's car. Why did they come here?

Amanda grabbed the door handle.

"You really want to go after them?" Judd asked. "In a graveyard? At night?"

"Yes." Amanda tugged at the handle. Still locked.

Judd's mouth curved up in a little smile. "Aren't you scared of ghosts?"

He's teasing me, Amanda realized. Playing with

me, like a cat with a mouse. "Don't be silly," she replied, forcing herself to laugh. "Unlock the doors, okay? You can leave if you want. I'll get a ride back with Janine."

Judd shook his head. "I'll come with you."

"Fine." Amanda wasn't about to argue. She tightened her grip on the door handle. "Let's go."

As soon as Judd popped the main lock, Amanda flung the door open, scrambled out of the car, and flew across the street.

"Hey!" Judd shouted behind her. "Amanda, wait!"

Amanda didn't slow down. She raced into the cemetery, following the path she and Janine had taken before.

"Amanda!" Judd's voice called. "Come on, wait up!"

Amanda could hear him sloshing along the path behind her. She tried to pick up her pace, even though the mud sucked at her shoes with every step.

"Amanda!" Judd's voice sounded farther behind her now.

She felt a surge of hope. If I can get to Janine, we can run out the other side of the cemetery, she thought. Find a house and use the phone to call the police.

Then what? she wondered. What will we tell them? That Judd is possessed by an evil spirit? No way will they believe it.

Worry about that later, she told herself. Just catch up with Janine and get out of here!

As she rounded a curve in the path, Amanda finally saw Janine up ahead, pointing at Sarah Fear's empty grave. Brandon stood beside her, gazing down at the gaping hole.

Janine turned when she heard Amanda's footsteps, a startled expression on her face. "Amanda! What are you doing here?"

Amanda grabbed her arm and pulled her aside. "It's Judd," she announced breathlessly. "I know it is."

Janine frowned in confusion.

"The Evil is inside Judd!" Amanda cried. "He left me a note and said I'm next. What are we going to do?"

Janine's face grew pale. Her brown eyes widened in fear as she glanced over Amanda's shoulder.

Amanda spun around.

Judd stood on the path.

"I heard you, Amanda." His voice sent a chill up Amanda's spine. "I heard every word."

Chapter 25

GRABBED BY THE EVIL

"*E*very single word," Judd repeated. Anger made his voice harsh. His blue eyes burned coldly.

I'm next, Amanda thought, remembering the note. Her heart pounded in rhythm with the words. I'm next. I'm next.

Judd clenched his fists and began moving toward her.

Amanda backed up a step, closer to the grave.

"How could you say that about me?" he demanded.

Amanda stepped back again. She quickly glanced over her shoulder. The empty grave stretched out behind her.

Judd kept coming, his angry eyes burning into her. He lifted his hands and uncurled his long fingers, reaching for her.

Amanda screamed.

"Get away from her!" Janine shouted. She grabbed Amanda's arm and yanked her to the side. "Brandon!" she cried. "Help us!"

"Yes. I will." Brandon turned away from the grave and raised his head.

Amanda gasped.

Brandon's eyes glowed golden-green like a cat's in the dark. An eerie, supernatural green that radiated evil.

Evil! Amanda's mouth went dry as terror shot through her.

It's Brandon. The Evil is inside Brandon.

"I will help you," Brandon repeated.

Why didn't I think of it? Amanda asked herself. Brandon walked in beside Judd the night we called up the Evil. Brandon killed Luke so that he could be the starting player. And Natalie must have told Brandon she was going to talk to the principal. So he killed her too.

Brandon's glowing eyes gazed back and forth between Amanda and Janine. "Thank you for calling me up," he told them. "But now I have no choice."

"What do you mean?" Janine's fingers dug painfully into Amanda's arm. "What are you talking about?"

"I must send you both to your graves!" The glow in Brandon's eyes grew stronger. "You first, Amanda."

Amanda's throat closed up in terror as his green eyes loomed closer, filling her vision. Janine screamed and tried to pull Amanda away.

Both of them stumbled, falling to their knees in the muddy ground.

140

Brandon began to close in on them.

"Nooo!" Judd shouted. He sprang through the air and landed on Brandon's back. His fingers clawed at Brandon's shoulders and neck.

Brandon shook himself like a wet dog. Judd slipped to the side, but managed to hang on. He grabbed a fistful of Brandon's red hair and yanked viciously.

Brandon hardly flinched.

Judd clamped his other hand over Brandon's face, his fingers digging into the flesh. "Run!" he shouted to Amanda and Janine. "Get out of here!"

Janine and Amanda struggled to their feet. Holding on to each other, they began to edge their way around the two boys.

Brandon reached up and grabbed Judd's wrists, then bent forward and dragged him over his head.

Judd hit the ground hard, landing flat on his back in front of Janine and Amanda.

Amanda cried out and reached out to help him up.

But Judd rolled away and jumped quickly to his feet. "Run!" he shouted again. Then he dived at Brandon.

Brandon caught him in midair. Holding Judd over his head, he spun around, then heaved him through the air.

Judd's body slammed up against a tree, then dropped to the ground.

He didn't get up again.

"Judd!" Amanda cried. She spun to Brandon. "You killed him!" she screamed. "You killed him!"

"Amanda, come on!" Janine pleaded, yanking at Amanda's sleeve. "Hurry! We have to get out of here!"

"Too late!" With a shout, Brandon knocked Janine aside and grabbed for Amanda. "You're next," he growled.

Chapter 26

IT CAN'T BE DROWNED

*B*randon's hands grasped for her throat.

Amanda ducked and dodged sideways.

His fingers brushed her hair, and she screamed in terror.

"Your turn, Amanda." Brandon snagged the back of her sweater. "Your turn."

"No!" Amanda twisted violently away and lost her balance, falling on her side into the mud. "Janine! Help me!"

Janine uttered a low moan.

She must have hit her head, Amanda thought frantically. She's dazed, she can't help!

Brandon stalked toward her, reaching for her again.

Amanda rolled onto her back and kicked out with her legs. Brandon grabbed an ankle, but she kicked up with the other foot and cracked him under the chin.

His jaw snapped shut on his tongue. Blood spurted from between his lips. He cried out in pain and his grip loosened on Amanda's ankle.

She kicked out again, then rolled over onto her knees and tried to rise.

Her feet slipped in the mud and she began to crawl away, sobbing in fear. "Janine!" she cried. "Get up! Can you get up?"

"What's . . . what's going on?" Janine's voice sounded weak and confused. "Amanda?"

"He's going to kill me!" Amanda sobbed, scrambling through the mud on her hands and knees. "Help me!"

"It's too late!" Brandon's footsteps splashed through the mud as he stormed after her. "It's your turn, Amanda. There's nothing you can do!"

"No!" Amanda scrambled to her feet and raced around to the head of the empty grave. Brandon stood at its foot, glaring at her.

A pink froth of blood bubbled from his mouth. He sucked it in and swallowed, licking his lips. "There's nothing you can do," he repeated. "Nowhere to go. No one to help."

Amanda stared at him, her breath coming in ragged sobs.

"You can't win, Amanda. You can't beat me." His eyes glowed triumphantly. "I will live forever."

No! Amanda thought, suddenly remembering. The Evil *can* be beat.

It must be drowned.

She glanced around and her heart sank. We're in the middle of a graveyard, she thought. There's no way to drown him. Not here.

A movement behind Brandon caught Amanda's

eye. Janine. She was on her feet now, moving toward Brandon.

Brandon heard her. He spun around and grabbed Janine, lifting her from the ground as if she weighed almost nothing. He pinned her arms to her side.

Janine cried out once, then gasped as he began squeezing the air from her lungs.

"Stop it!" Amanda screamed.

She had to do something. Glancing around frantically, she spotted a fallen branch. She grabbed it up and ran around the grave.

Holding the branch like a baseball bat, Amanda swung it over her shoulder, then brought it crashing against the back of Brandon's skull with a loud crack.

Brandon howled. A shudder passed through him.

His grip loosened, and Janine dropped to the ground in heap. Shaking his head to clear it, Brandon staggered sideways toward the grave.

The grave! Amanda thought quickly. If we can push him in there, maybe . . . maybe he'll go back in time.

"Help me, Janine!" Amanda shouted. She grabbed hold of Janine's arm and hauled her to her feet. "We can't drown the Evil, but maybe we can send it away. Help me push him in the grave."

Janine gazed at her blankly.

Brandon stopped and turned toward them.

"Come on, Janine!" Amanda screamed. "Help me shove him into the grave before it's too late!"

As Amanda swung the branch at Brandon again, Janine finally seemed to understand. She ran up and shoved him.

Brandon danced back out of their way. But Amanda kept swinging the branch, cracking him in the knees, then in the side of the head. As Brandon swung his arm out, trying to grab hold of the branch, Janine shoved him hard.

Brandon dodged back. His heel slid over the edge of the grave. He caught his balance and began to lunge forward.

Switching her grip on the branch, Amanda held it like a battering ram—and drove it straight into his chest.

Brandon teetered for a second, then toppled backward into the open coffin.

Amanda peered over the edge.

Brandon lay still. His eyes were closed, shutting out their eerie green glow.

"He's unconscious! Quick! Close the lid!" Amanda cried. She and Janine ran around to the left of the grave. The lid rested against one side of the grave, stuck in the muddy earth.

"Use the branch," Janine suggested quickly. "Pry it loose with the branch."

Amanda stuck the branch down, but it was too thick to slip between the coffin lid and the wall of earth. She glanced around for something thinner.

Her gaze landed on Judd, lying crumpled and still beneath the tree. Tears rose to her eyes. I thought he was possessed by the Evil, she remembered guiltily. How could I have been so wrong?

A twig snapped.

Amanda stiffened.

Janine grasped Amanda's wrist. Her fingers were icy. She tried to speak, but no sound came out.

Slowly, Amanda turned her gaze to where Janine was staring.

A woman stood a few feet from the end of the grave.

Half corpse. Half skeleton.

146

Decaying flesh hung in strips from her face. Her lips were black with rot. Her hands dangled at her sides. The long finger bones gleamed, picked clean of skin and meat.

"Sarah Fear," Amanda whispered. But which Sarah was it? The real Sarah—the one who drowned on the way to London? Or Jane, who had taken Sarah's name when they switched places?

"What's going on?" Janine cried. "I thought the Evil was inside Brandon! Why is Sarah Fear here?"

The hideous corpse stood quietly, staring at them with empty eye sockets. And then she staggered forward, toward Amanda and Janine.

She raised her arms, and pieces of tattered material fell away, exposing rotting flesh and shiny bone.

The corpse took another staggering step. Her bony fingers curled like claws as she reached out for Amanda.

"Leave me alone!" Amanda cried. "Don't hurt me!"

Chapter 27

GOOD-BYE, AMANDA AND BRANDON

*T*he corpse took another lurching step.

Its bones creaked and rattled. Clumps of blackened flesh fell from its arms and plopped softly into the mud.

Amanda screamed again. She backed away and bumped into Janine, who stood frozen now, too frightened to move.

The corpse reached the end of the grave.

The overpowering smell of rotting flesh filled the air. Amanda swallowed hard and covered her mouth with her hand. "Come on!" she choked out, giving Janine a tug. "We have to get out of here. Hurry!"

Amanda tugged again, and Janine finally responded. They dodged away from the bony, grasping fingers and ran up to the head of the grave.

The corpse stopped and turned her head from side to side. The neck bones creaked like rusty hinges.

"We can't leave Judd here!" Amanda cried. "We have to take him with us somehow. If we leave him, who knows what she might do to him?"

Janine shuddered and squeezed Amanda's hand. "Okay. Let's go."

The corpse started to move again. It took one lurching step around the corner of the grave.

Amanda and Janine began to run down the opposite side.

A howl of pure rage suddenly split the air.

They stopped dead. The howl echoed in the night.

"What *was* that?" Janine cried.

Before Amanda could answer, Brandon sprang from the coffin and landed at the foot of the grave. His eyes gleamed stronger than ever, lighting up the hideous face of the corpse with their eerie green glow.

The corpse turned. As her empty gaze seemed to focus on Brandon, her rotting lips drew back in a snarl. "No!" she shouted. Her voice sounded like a young woman's. "Not you! You're dead. I killed you!"

"You thought you did. But you failed!" Bellowing in fury, Brandon leaped through the air and attacked the corpse. His powerful hand closed around her arm, snapping the bone.

The corpse shrieked in agony and twisted away. "I killed you, Sarah!" she screamed again. "You were supposed to stay dead!"

"Never!" Brandon yelled. "I'll never die!"

The corpse hissed like a snake and raked her hand over Brandon's face.

Blood seeped out of the cuts and trickled into Brandon's eyes.

"You'll die now!" the corpse shrieked. She clawed at Brandon's chest, ripping his shirt and leaving a trail of bloody cuts in his skin.

"What's going on?" Janine screamed. "What's happening?"

Amanda suddenly realized the truth. "The corpse isn't Sarah!" she cried. "It isn't the real Sarah. It's Jane Hardy!"

"What are you talking about?" Janine demanded.

"Sarah's spirit possessed Jane a hundred years ago, and now it's in Brandon. But Jane is still trying to kill it! She—"

A horrible shriek interrupted Amanda.

Still struggling, Brandon and Jane stood at the very edge of the grave.

Jane kept ripping at Brandon's flesh with the sharp bones of her fingers. Strips of skin hung from his face like bloody ribbons, and he shrieked in pain.

"Die!" Jane screamed. She lurched forward, trying to shove him into the gaping hole. "Die!"

The Evil in Brandon howled in rage. "I'm not going down into that grave again. Never again!" He swung his arm, punching his fist into the side of Jane's skull.

Pieces of rotting flesh flew from her face. She rocked back, stunned.

"Never!" Brandon shouted. "Never!"

Jane snarled and tore at him again.

Brandon dodged her ripping, clawlike hand. His foot slid in the mud.

Jane rushed at him, shoving him from behind. But Brandon caught his balance and dug his heels in.

The Evil is too strong, Amanda thought. Jane will never be able to push it into the grave.

Not alone.

Help her, she told herself. Help her shove it in and bury the Evil forever.

Taking a deep breath, Amanda rushed toward the struggling corpse.

"What are you doing?" Janine screamed. "Stop!"

Amanda couldn't stop. Brandon was wheeling around, grabbing for Jane's neck. In another second, his powerful hands would snap her head off.

As Brandon reached for Jane's throat, Amanda plowed into him. Shoved him backward.

His glowing eyes widened in surprise.

His heels slipped over the edge of the grave.

Amanda cried out—and pushed at him again.

Roaring in anger, Brandon fell back.

His feet slid off the edge of the grave. He swung an arm out wildly.

His fingers locked around Amanda's wrist.

"No!" she screamed. She grabbed at his fingers, desperately trying to pry them loose.

But Brandon held her in a ferocious grip.

And as he fell into the grave, he pulled Amanda in with him.

PART FIVE

Chapter 28

THEY BOTH DROWN

*A*manda smiled to herself as a soft, warm breeze washed over her. Nice, she thought. So comfortable.

She turned on her side to snuggle deeper into the pillow.

The mattress felt as hard and solid as a slab of wood.

Scowling, Amanda opened her eyes.

Darkness surrounded her.

She sat up, bracing herself on one elbow. How did the bed get so hard?

The bed tilted. Amanda's elbow scraped along the hard surface. She put her other hand down to keep her balance.

It's not a bed, she realized. It *is* wood. Am I on a floor?

The breeze grew cooler and stronger. And damp. Amanda could feel the sticky moisture on her skin.

The floor tilted again.

Birds screeched overhead.

The darkness began to fade, and Amanda heard the sound of voices. Men and women, shouting anxiously, calling out to each other in troubled tones.

Above their cries, Amanda heard the voices of two women, shouting furiously.

The darkness faded further. Amanda saw a cloudy sky and a trio of gulls swooping overhead. She heard water, slapping hard at the floor, making it pitch sideways.

Not a floor, she realized.

A boat. I'm on a boat.

The women's voices grew louder. Angrier. "It should have been you!" one of them cried.

Amanda turned her head toward the sound.

Two young women stood near the railing across the deck from Amanda, facing each other. Both wore high-buttoned boots and old-fashioned dresses with long skirts. They wore their hair piled high on their heads, with silk ribbons twisted through it.

One woman had fiery red hair. The other's was a light, silky brown.

Jane and Sarah.

They're young again! Amanda thought. Alive and young. Back in their bodies, exactly the way they were when I saw them switch identities.

Except they're not at the carriage house, planning the switch. They're on a boat. And they're fighting.

Amanda glanced around.

Men in straw hats and women in long dresses stood

along the railings, gazing fearfully into the churning water.

A wave rose up. The ship rose with it, then dropped down. An icy sheet of water surged across the deck.

Voices cried out in terror. "We're in for it now!" a man shouted.

Amanda gasped at the words. I'm on the same ship, she thought, suddenly understanding. When Brandon pulled me into the grave, we went back in time.

And now I'm on the same ship I saw when I fell into the grave before.

This is where Sarah died.

This is where the Evil was born.

The ship rose up again. It seemed to hang in the air forever. Then it slammed back down with a jolt, shuddering and creaking as it hit.

People screamed and clutched the railings. "We're in for it now!" the man shouted again.

The ship's about to sink, Amanda realized. Just like the last time.

But this time it's different.

This time Jane is here too.

Glancing around again, Amanda spotted a young man curled up against the railing a few feet away. He wore jeans, a blue plaid shirt, and black, high-topped sneakers. His red hair ruffled in the wind.

Brandon!

Of course, Amanda thought. We both went back through time.

Amanda gazed at him anxiously. He appeared to be sleeping. His brows drew together in a frown, then smoothed out again. His eyelashes cast feathery shadows on his face.

His face! Amanda realized. It's whole again. No cuts. No bloody strips of skin hanging down. He looks the way he always did.

He's not possessed by the Evil anymore.

The Evil hasn't been born yet.

Amanda called his name, but Brandon didn't respond.

A scream of rage and frustration pierced the air. Amanda turned back to Sarah and Jane. The waves had drenched their boots and skirts. The wind had blown their hair down. It whipped around their faces in wet, ropy strands.

They didn't notice. Their anger was too strong.

"It should have been you!" Sarah screamed at Jane. "This was your fate, not mine!"

"And you've been getting your revenge ever since!" Jane shouted back. "You possessed me. You killed my husband, Thomas. You killed so many people! I have been trying to stop you ever since. And now I will stop you forever!"

"Never!" Sarah gave Jane a shove and turned to run.

Jane caught her by the hair and pulled her back. Screaming in pain and fury, Sarah broke loose. She spun around and grabbed at Jane's neck.

"You were supposed to die here!" Sarah screamed. "This is where I drowned, pretending to be you." Her fingers dug into Jane's throat. "But *you* were the one who was supposed to die. You didn't deserve to be happy and alive. *I* should have lived!"

Sarah tightened her grip on Jane's throat. Jane's eyes grew wide. She whipped her head back and forth, struggling to breathe.

"Never!" Sarah kept shouting. "You'll never stop me!"

I have to do something, Amanda thought. I can't let Sarah win again!

As she began to stand, another wave tossed the ship, knocking her to her knees again. She rolled onto her side and glanced across the deck, gasping with relief.

The wave had knocked Jane and Sarah apart too. Jane was alive, breathing.

Sarah hadn't won yet.

Jane grabbed Sarah by the arms. Sarah tried to break free, but Jane held on. "This time I *will* die here," Jane screamed into Sarah's face. "I'll drown you before your Evil can kill anyone! This time we will *both* die here!"

"Nooo!" Sarah thrashed and twisted in Jane's grip. "I don't want to die!"

The ship rose up and crashed down, tilting dangerously. People screamed in terror and fought their way to the high side of the deck, clinging to the railing as the icy water washed over them.

No one seemed to notice the two young women as they staggered across the tilting deck.

"I don't want to die!" Sarah shrieked. "I never had a chance to live!"

The ship tilted farther. A wave washed over the deck, its force throwing Sarah and Jane against the railing. They leaned against it, still wrestling.

Amanda began to slide, down toward Sarah and Jane and the foaming water. She dug in with all her strength and crawled her way up the slanting deck to Brandon.

He was sitting up now, one hand grasping the

railing. He used the other to wipe water from his face. Then he blinked, glancing around in confusion.

"Brandon!" Amanda cried, pulling herself up next to him.

"Amanda?" Brandon blinked again, dazed. The strange green glow had disappeared from his eyes. "What happened? I feel so weird."

"I know." Amanda scooted closer to him.

"Where are we? Are we on a boat?" Brandon asked. Amanda nodded.

"What's going on?"

"The ship is sinking. But we'll be okay. I've been through this before—I don't think our bodies are really here."

"What?" Brandon cried. "What do you mean?"

Before Amanda could reply, a scream of pure terror rose above the sound of the water and the cries of the passengers.

Amanda gazed down at Sarah and Jane.

The ship had listed even farther. Sarah and Jane were on their sides. Only the railing kept them from tumbling into the ocean inches below.

"I never had a chance to live!" Sarah screamed again. She struggled frantically to break loose from Jane. "Nooo!"

Jane gritted her teeth and hung on to Sarah's arms, her face twisted in determination and fury.

She's scared, but she won't let go, Amanda thought. She's determined to kill Sarah.

To kill the Evil for good.

A huge wave rose up and crashed against the slanting deck. Amanda put her arms around Brandon and watched in horror as the wave fell back, washing Jane and Sarah overboard.

Sarah's head came up immediately. Water streamed from her hair and into her mouth as she thrashed in the churning ocean.

She went under, then bobbed back up, screaming.

As Sarah struggled in the water, Jane rose to the surface. She reached out her hand, grabbed Sarah's hair, and pulled her back under.

Huddled next to Brandon, Amanda waited, scanning the water.

Jane and Sarah didn't come up again.

Chapter 29

NO MORE EVIL?

*A*manda didn't dare take her eyes off the water.

The Evil is so powerful, she thought. Can it really be killed? Can it be drowned?

Keep watching, she ordered herself.

Amanda's eyes burned. She wanted to close them and drift off to sleep, but she didn't dare.

She had to watch out for the Evil.

Her eyelids drooped. Her head sank onto her knees. She snapped it up, gasping. Had she been asleep? How long?

Amanda rubbed her eyes and gazed out at the water again.

Still no sign of the Evil.

But you can't stop watching, Amanda thought.

Her eyelids drooped again. She fought against it,

tried to keep them open. Don't go to sleep, she told herself.

Her head sank forward.

Don't go to sleep.

Her eyes closed.

"Don't!" Amanda cried out. She tried to move and felt a hand grip her shoulder.

"Amanda?" a voice murmured.

Janine's voice.

With a gasp, Amanda opened her eyes.

Janine stood over her, gazing down anxiously. "Thank goodness you woke up."

"Huh?" Amanda stared at her friend, confused.

"Do you hurt or something?" Janine asked. "Do you need some medicine?"

"What do you . . ." Amanda broke off, suddenly realizing that she was lying in a bed. Not her bed, though. The mattress felt different and the pillow was hard.

She glanced around. Metal rails on the side of the bed. A television hanging from the ceiling. A funny smell.

Medicine.

Amanda snapped her gaze back to Janine. "I'm in the hospital, aren't I?"

Janine nodded, a concerned expression on her face. "Are you sure you don't want me to get the nurse?" she asked.

"No, I'm okay." Amanda spotted a little metal box near her hand. She punched a button and the bed slowly rose up to a sitting position. "What happened?" she asked. "How did I get here? Where's Brandon?"

"The police found you—in the Fear Street Cemetery. You and Brandon." Janine pulled a yellow plastic chair close to the bed and sat down. "You were both unconscious. And your clothes were soaking wet."

Amanda blinked, remembering the icy waves washing across the deck.

"We were all so scared," Janine declared, squeezing Amanda's hand gently. "What were you two doing at the cemetery? What happened to you? Were you attacked?"

Amanda squinted hard at her. "Don't you remember?"

"Remember what?"

"The Evil!" Amanda cried.

Janine stared at her, her round face full of confusion. "The . . . the what?"

"The Evil!" Amanda repeated. "I thought it was inside Judd, but it wasn't. It was inside Brandon all the time. It killed Luke and Natalie. We were all at Sarah Fear's grave, fighting the Evil! Remember?"

Janine bit her lip. "Amanda, I don't know what you're talking about. I think maybe I should get the doctor."

"Are you kidding me?" Amanda narrowed her eyes. "Are you *pretending* you don't remember?"

"No! I wouldn't do that to you!" Janine protested. "I just don't understand what you are saying. Luke and Natalie are perfectly fine."

Amanda gazed at her.

Did it all happen?

Has something tricked Janine's memory?

Or was it all some kind of nightmare fantasy?

Janine smiled at Amanda. "I guess you had some

really horrible dreams while you were unconscious. Evil and graves and somebody named Sarah." She reached for the plastic pitcher on the bedside table. "Want some water?"

"No!" Amanda almost shouted, sitting up straight. Janine froze, her hand on the pitcher.

"Do you remember *anything?*" Amanda demanded. "What about the box I found in Corky Corcoran's locker? You're the one who read the letter and the instructions on how to call up the Evil. You have to remember that!"

"I don't know what you're talking about," Janine repeated. "I'm sorry, Amanda. You said we were at Sarah Fear's grave, but I never heard of Sarah Fear. You and Brandon were found in a part of the cemetery that hasn't even been used yet."

This isn't true, Amanda thought. It can't be. "What about the box? Corky's box?" she demanded.

Janine shook her head. "I don't know. I don't remember any box. I never heard anything about this Evil. And believe me, no one has been killed."

Amanda fell back against the bed, stunned.

"So what happened to you and Brandon?" Janine asked again. "Your parents are worried sick. They went down to the cafeteria for coffee. They'll be right back up. I think—"

"I have to see Brandon," Amanda interrupted. "Right away. Is he okay? Is he here?"

"He recovered quickly," Janine replied. "But he says he doesn't remember what happened to you two. He's been waiting with me outside."

"Bring him in," Amanda demanded. "Please— hurry."

Looking puzzled, Janine disappeared.

A few seconds later, Brandon entered. "Are you okay?" he asked, studying her thoughtfully.

"Are you?" she replied.

He nodded and took the chair by her bed.

"Our parents are all having cows!" Brandon declared. "I really don't know what to tell them. I mean, about what happened to us."

Did it happen? Amanda wondered.

Did I dream it? I have to ask him. I have to know.

"Brandon?" She cleared her throat nervously. "Do you remember being on the ship with me?"

He leaned close and whispered his reply. "I don't think I'll ever forget it."

"Thank goodness!" Amanda cried. "Janine thinks I dreamed the whole thing."

"It wasn't a dream," Brandon assured her. "You and I sat together on that sinking ship and watched those two young women drown in the ocean. It—it was so horrifying . . ." His voice trailed off.

"Yes, it was," Amanda agreed. "I kept watching the water. I was so afraid they would come back up."

Brandon shook his head. "They didn't. We saw them drown."

"And the Evil drowned with them," Amanda said thoughtfully. "That's why Natalie and Luke are alive. They didn't die because the Evil drowned with Sarah and Jane."

Brandon nodded. "We watched it drown. Now Sarah and Jane can rest peacefully."

Amanda sighed.

Brandon took her hand. "But *we* can't rest peacefully—can we, Amanda?" He leaned closer, and his eyes glowed bright green. Such an evil, unnatural green.

166

"No. We can't rest," Amanda agreed, squeezing his hand. She pulled herself up. And stared back at him, her eyes glowing green, as bright and evil as his.

She felt the Evil pulsing inside her. Throbbing . . . throbbing so powerfully. Sarah and Jane drowned. But the Evil didn't drown with them . . .

"We can't rest," Amanda repeated, squeezing Brandon's hand tighter, tighter. "You and I have so much work to do!'

About the Author

R.L. Stine is the best-selling author in America. He has written over one hundred scary books for young people, all of them bestsellers.

His series include *Fear Street, Ghosts of Fear Street* and the *Fear Street Sagas.*

Bob grew up in Columbus, Ohio. Today he lives in New York City with his wife, Jane, his teenage son, Matt, and his dog, Nadine.